Leslie Sir ...

a work that pr ... . step in the essential discourse for transforming the Israeli Palestinian conflict. The characters are riveting, real and narrate the story through lives lived on a daily basis...The writing is captivating, so much so that I can hear the charged ferocity and feel the thrust of the pain throughout. Through the lives of the sisters, possibilities evolve that we all need to consider.

Daphne Muse, Writer and former director
of the Women's Leadership Institute, Mills College

The Divine Comic is an **engrossing**, powerful descent into the agony of American Jews trying to come to grips with a shattered dream. It's a close study of a family with a past rooted in radical, anarchist and communist politics, haunted by the Nazi mass murders, and wrestling with their dismay over Israel's treatment of the Palestinians. The narrator, who travels to the Middle East to meet Israelis and Palestinians, reaches the conclusion that she must reject Israel's occupation and Zionism but she has to reach out to her sister who has a history of angry rejections and whose own anguish pushes her close to suicide. The conflict unfolds, as it often does, at each Passover as the family comes together. These aren't the usual family get-together blow-ups; instead, these are the arguments of a very politically aware liberal Jewish family thrown into crisis...Leslie Simon presents their tension with wit and insight. *The Divine Comic* is a rare book, dramatizing a transformation of attitudes that affects all Americans deeply.

HILTON OBENZINGER, AUTHOR OF *BUSY DYING* AND *TREYF PESACH*, WINNER OF THE AMERICAN BOOK AWARD, AND ASSOCIATE DIRECTOR OF THE CHINESE RAILROAD WORKERS IN NORTH AMERICA PROJECT, STANFORD UNIVERSITY

The readers of Leslie Simon's novel *The Divine Comic* will quickly feel at home with the deftly drawn characters who also embody the theme of the necessity of dialogue, of sincere, plucky efforts toward reconciliation and peace. Two of the major characters, the two sisters, Beatrice and Leah, stand for integrity/justice versus security—justice for the Palestinians, who are made homeless in their own home and security for the indigenous as well as the Holocaust-driven Jewish immigrant populations. Ultimately, the basis of this conflict boils down to those two words. Do those two words/values always have to be on a collision course? Simon's novel offers the hope, persuasively, that this either-or fallacy can be overcome. With *The Divine Comic*, Simon has raised the genre of political novel to unparalleled heights. I look forward to using this novel as a required text in my class on American Cultures in Literature and Film. I have been waiting for such a book for a long time.

ABDUL JABBAR, PROFESSOR EMERITUS,
CITY COLLEGE OF SAN FRANCISCO

THE DIVINE COMIC

Leslie Simon

SPUYTEN DUYVIL
New York City

This is a work of fiction. Names, characters, businesses, places, events, locales, and incidents are either the products of the author's imagination or used in a fictitious manner. Any resemblance to actual persons, living or dead, is purely coincidental.

Library of Congress Cataloging-in-Publication Data

Names: Simon, Leslie, 1947- author. | Morales, Aurora Levins, other.
Title: The divine comic / Leslie Simon, Aurora Levins Morales.
Description: New York City : Spuyten Duyvil, [2020]
Identifiers: LCCN 2020010733 | ISBN 9781949966992 (paperback)
Subjects: GSAFD: Historical fiction.
Classification: LCC PS3569.I4826 D58 2020 | DDC 813/.54--dc23
LC record available at https://lccn.loc.gov/2020010733

for Lena and Sam

Now, since it is a fact that love cannot
   ignore the welfare of its loving self,
   there's nothing in the world that can hate itself

Dante Alighieri
(translated by Mark Musa)
   The Divine Comedy: Purgatory, Canto XVII

Imagined voices, and beloved, too,
of those who died, or of those who are
lost unto us like the dead.

Sometimes in our dreams they speak to us;
sometimes in its thought the mind will hear them.

And with their sound for a moment there return
sounds from the first poetry of our life—
like music, in the night, far off, that fades away.

C. P. Cavafy "Voices"
(translated by Daniel Mendelsohn)
   Collected Poems

To be a Jew in the twentieth century
Is to be offered a gift. If you refuse,
Wishing to be invisible, you choose
Death of the spirit, the stone insanity.
Accepting, take full life.   Full agonies:
Your evening deep in labyrinthine blood
Of those who resist, fail, and resist; and God
Reduced to a hostage among hostages.

The gift is torment.   Not alone the still
Torture, isolation; or torture of the flesh.
That may come also.   But the accepting wish,
The whole and fertile spirit as guarantee
For every human freedom, suffering to be free,
Daring to live for the impossible.

Muriel Rukeyser from "Letter to the Front"
   Beast in View

FOREWORD:
WE LEARN THE WORLD THROUGH STORIES
AURORA LEVINS MORALES

I am a believer in the transformative power of art. Our world is constructed from stories, interpretations of reality that are our maps of the possible. All art is political in that it expresses some story about what matters, and who and how. Consciously political art does this on purpose, because to shift the story shifts what we imagine is possible, and that changes everything. What's possible can be worked for, defended, organized around, proposed, built, won.

Information alone doesn't have this power. To touch our dreams, to change us at the level of belief, we need the full spectrum of intellect and emotion, philosophical vision and sensuality, galaxies of broad cultural meaning and uniquely individual details of human experience that art provides.

I grew up in a home full of stories, a house lined with bookshelves, on a remote farm in the middle of a rainforest, a radical home where I read the poetry of Bertolt Brecht and Pablo Neruda and grew up singing the songs of the International Brigades that fought fascism in Spain in the 1930s. But more than anything else, I grew up in a world of novels. I would climb up into a tree, and surrounded by flame colored flowers and a cacophony of birds, bury myself in the pages of Robert Louis Stevenson's *Kidnapped* until it was time to climb down for lunch. Because I read voraciously and was a daydreamer, immersing myself in fictional worlds, I had a feel for many realities far removed from my own: rebellion in the Scottish Highlands, urban poverty in 19th century England, Chinese resistance to the Japanese invasion of WWII. I read about poor children walking across India for eye surgery, about white Australian kids riding boundaries in the outback, about Dutch children surviving floods and hiding in attics under Nazi occupation and children who were working artists in London between the World Wars.

One of my favorite books was Howard Fast's *Tony and the Wonderful Door*, in which a working class boy from 1930s Manhattan finds his way into the 18th century, where he meets and builds relationships with Native American and Dutch villagers, witnesses injustice and tries to do something about it, tells his truth and is disbelieved, and both wins and loses in the end. I loved that book for the magic, and the wonder, I loved it because Tony MacTavish Levy, a mixed heritage Jewish child like me, faced real ethical dilemmas and had an opportunity to test himself, to choose integrity, to fight hard for what mattered to him, and I loved it because there was a price to pay for courage, and that's real. I felt respected by the demands of the story.

Fictional people can draw us, through their imagined lives, to explore realities we shy away from in our non-fictional lives, to become familiar with the strange. They also give us private entry into terrible places we can't bear to approach directly, engage our hearts that are too well shielded to tremble in the numbing presence of the nightly news, lure us into opening our eyes.

Well-crafted political fiction invites into some of those terrible places, on the one hand giving us the emotional safety of knowing it's make-believe and on the other, the searing intimacy of the personal tale to make it all real again. Within the shelter of a novel, we can approach the pain of others and find our complex humanity and our hope. In novels, we fall in love with Haitian refugees dying on a raft, Dominican sisters we know will be murdered in the last chapter, dirt poor Southern white survivors of drunken beatings and incest. We want to be with them, to be told their secrets, to accompany them on their journeys. Absorbed by their inner and outer battles, we become part of a conversation the author has tricked us into, by entangling us with characters we can't turn away from.

The political novel is at its most powerful when it opens up a conversation that's been censored, stifled, driven into silence in the arenas of public debate, when it pulls back the veil over unpalatable truths, reveals humanity in those we've rejected, when it refuses to allow us to be numb. Sometimes, in moments of great conflict, what we need most is to feel deeply the realities of people we do and don't agree with, to feel the texture of the issues in their lives, to cultivate compassion and insight where there are only stances.

In U.S. Jewish life, in the early 21st century, there is no issue more polarized, where dissent is more likely to be censored and punished, than that of the Israeli-Palestinian conflict. People who openly oppose the crushing suppression and violence of the Israeli state toward the Palestinian people get death threats, lose funding for their organizations, have their lectures canceled. A friend of mine was pepper-sprayed at a meeting of his own peace organization. Using words like *occupation,* or even acknowledging that Palestinians exist, can get you put on lists, targeted for harassment, accused of self-hatred and retroactive collaboration with Nazi plans to exterminate the Jews. I myself appear twice on the Masada 2000 list of Self Hating/Israel Threatening Jews, (my Latin American double last name confused them) and because my poetry proclaims the lives of Palestinians to be as precious to me as the lives of Israeli Jews, I have been told that I have betrayed the ghosts of dead Jewish children, of my own relatives buried in trenches under Ukrainian farmland.

Most U.S, Jews don't spit on each other or call each other Nazis. But the Jewish right's fierce intolerance of dissent, the swift silencing of even the mildest critique of Israeli policies, the aggressive and well-organized campaigns to discredit individuals and organizations calling for human rights for Palestinians, all make it very hard to think independently, listen compassionately, or speak openly and without fear in our own communities and even in our families.

And those who insist that criticism of Israel be absolutely clean of the real, historical, Jew-hating baggage that still drips its venom into the nooks and crannies of progressive organizing, who love Israelis as people and say so, who worry about bombs on Jerusalem buses as well as white phosphorus in Gaza, are called collaborators or dupes, as if anti-Semitism really were just an Israeli hoax; are told it's inappropriate to be concerned about the wellbeing of Jews, that because Israel oppresses, Jews don't deserve to be safe, our right to life conditional on the policies of a government very few of us chose. To want everyone secure, sovereign, and at peace is cause for suspicion.

Into this thick and difficult wall, Leslie Simon has opened her own magical door, a novel of two dissenting sisters (and some kibitzing ghosts), estranged, entrenched in their positions, every bit as emotional and polarized as counter-demonstrators yelling at each other outside an Israeli embassy, and because she has given us fictional people to love, drawn us into their furious, aching hearts and the wild and semi-supernatural chatter in their heads, she's made it possible to be curious about what we disagree with, made us want to understand what makes them tick, brought us to the family dinner table, where we can sit down with the whole menu of anguished arguments and notice, in the midst of raised voices and waving hands, how much we yearn to find our way to each other.

With passion and humor, she has made a literary clearing where polemics take on flesh and personality and dreams, a place full of haunted pasts and family dinners, actual journeys and journeys of the broken heart. With the help of two highly articulate dead people, she constructs and shatters her heroine's certainties, taking us deeper and deeper into these women's lives, making us listen, softening the hard places, until we are no longer spectators, until our own stories, the ones we each hold in our bones, in our bellies, about these two peoples, this one land, this war and all its long roots, until our own stories can no longer sit still, until they push aside the empty plates, the dregs of wine, lean forward, still listening, elbows on the tablecloth, hearts in our throats, and speak.

2008

My sister had a plan, and she intended to act on it. I started getting hot, so I opened a window. Then I heard it. Chopin. Leah had planned to die to Chopin. A good choice, I thought, as I climbed out the window.

If you saw us walking in Chicago down a Jackson Park path, or along Venice Beach in Los Angeles, you would know we were sisters. The beauty. And the funny looking one, who managed the luck of no beauty so well. You wouldn't notice how little we looked alike.

Though I love my baby sister, our arguments line up one Passover Seder after another.

No one hates a Jew more than another Jew.

My friend Danny understood the problem of the self against the self. That's why he tried to make friends again of the two sisters. The beauty, and the one who loved her oh so well. Danny Gonzalez, the wisest comic this side of Lenny Bruce.

DANNY'S DAY

I'd gotten used to Danny, who appeared about a year after he died. We'd grown up together, went to high school, college. Even made love one night. His one and only with a girl. He told me it didn't convince him to convert, but it shot way above his expectations. "My little bird, my best friend," he whispered. But even though the sex didn't last, I could coast into the idea that he'd stick around. And he did, until he died. Then, to my surprise, pleasure, and anxious disbelief, on the afternoon of New Year's Eve, in 1983, he arranged his comeback, at the twins' seventh birthday party.

You think you were done with me? Well, you thought wrong, my little bird.

Neither brilliant nor beautiful, I came into the world without much physical grace or ability to draw. Not even an ear for music or the gift of pronouncing foreign languages correctly. Luckily, people seemed to like me. I had a talent for friendship. In fact, that's how I got into the Girls Chorus in high school. Just trying to support my friend with the voice of a lark, a nightingale, an angel– *you* name it–but no self-confidence, I accompanied her to the audition at the beginning of freshman year. Since Mr. Kleinz assumed I had come to try out, I thought *Why not?* And, then, once Jeanie stopped shaking and started singing, she impressed him as the best pick of our class. He could see her breezing into one solo after another as our four years rolled on. So he made the supportive teacher move and let me in, too. Curtsy tails, you might call it, except that curtsies had started to fade out; even girls had learned how to take their bows. Anyway, my admission to the Girls Chorus had strict conditions. Too bad the Mixed Chorus director didn't have such a big heart. I'd have preferred to look across the stage at George Lukovic and mouth the words from the soprano section. I had been diagnosed an alto, but, hey, if you're mouthing the words, does it matter where you stand?

At Brennan High School on the South Side of Chicago, the Serbs dominated the football team, and Lukovic, the quarterback, collected crushes from lots of girls, even some of the Jewish ones, like me. The black kids ran the basketball team, and the Jews edited the school newspaper. Stereotypes you could call them. Niches. Slots. Unfair? Sure. And my dad railed against the tracking system and a few other things. He got even angrier after my mom died.

My family's own private holocaust. Not like the mother whose ex-husband murdered her four children and then himself, not like the single mother whose only child committed suicide, not like the girl whose parents and brother burned to death in a fire, and not like the bigger ones—the Jews in Europe, the Africans dragged to America, the people already here, and countless others in their own countries, including ones the average person never hears about, like the disappeared girls in Ciudad Juárez, which makes me think about the Mexicans at Brennan. They never had a niche, except Danny, who made his own niche, everywhere he went.

Enough with the holocausts, mi chicanita.

4

Danny, I'm not Chicana. Don't you think you're disrespecting the term?

And you think enough with the holocausts *is a* Mexican *expression?*

Danny always had his *movidas*, a word he taught me in eighth grade. As the oldest child in the Gonzalez family, the only Mexicans on our side of the viaduct, which sat under the Chicago Skyway as it blew by on its way to East Chicago and Gary, Indiana, Danny learned early that comedy might help him live longer. After all, in a tragedy no one leaves the stage alive. He didn't count on AIDS. None of us did.

In college I slept with Gracie, the girl in the dorm room across the hall, for a while, and Danny fell in love with Antonio. This is a modern story. About an ancient land. One of God's beauties. The land between the Dead and the Med Seas. Israel or Palestine, depending on the angle of your eye. Which promise you signed on for. Well, Gracie and I parted like another body of water in the region, but Danny kept his eyes on the boys, and one of them gave him AIDS. Early on. He died in 1982, the year Mitch and I split up. A bad year? You could say.

Anyway, a year later Danny came back. I think mostly to help me with my sister. Our own private civil war. By 35, I had a career, a loving, though bewildered ex-husband, two healthy children, the source of my great happiness and intermittent feelings of stability, and a sister whose life I barely understood.

Mom died the fall Leah turned thirteen. Six years older and already in my sophomore year at college, I never experienced the lonesomeness of our old house with just my father and my sister knocking around in it. Sure, I faced the emptiness when I came home for breaks, but back at school I could somehow pretend that Mom, like everyone else in the family, still slept at night at 8813 Paxton Avenue, woke up, ate breakfast, talked on the phone to friends, went shopping. I could imagine her going to class at Chicago Teachers College so she could fulfill her dream. But when I arrived home for college breaks, her absence knocked me over. After she died, Dad's heart broke, and then he threw himself into trying to find another mother for Leah. When he realized that he could find lovers, perhaps a companion for his old age, but that no one could replace Mom in any of our lives, his grief became complete, not finished, not done, but pure. Nothing would change his sorrow, not even all the joys he would later experience. His life, not over, not even ruined, made it around a corner he wouldn't notice until he had gone too far, and love, except for the love for his children and grandchildren, became a memory, distant, along with anticipation and other earthly gifts.

As for Leah, when I came home from college that first Thanksgiving after Mom died, I could see that something had happened to her. Unlike Dad, who soaked himself in memory, she started losing hers. I tried to tell her stories about Mom, but she didn't want to hear them.

Okay, I know we have to concentrate on Leah here, but when are you going to tell them about my day, already? That's the name of this chapter, after all.

Danny, I want to do it right. Poetic, prophetic.

Pathetic, mija.

Let me just try, all right?

6

Go for it, but get to the good stuff before you put them to sleep.

Okay. Danny's Day. I shall deliver it with style.

Winter had kept on tugging at everyone's nerves acting like it would not let up, pushing its case with a light snowfall at the equinox in March and delivering ten inches on April Fool's Day. You can imagine the jokes. Then it happened. That fresh spring where the air sweeps you into its arms, promising love and flowers. Tulips popping open in front yard planters, lilacs brushing backyard fences, people on buses acting friendly, happy to wait for their turn to board so they could stare out at the trees in all their new bushy, blossomy glory. Danny called it "a spring well-done."

And though I see you have swallowed someone else's voice, I like your attempt at embellishment.

Danny, please *shush* for a moment. Let me indulge as I divulge.

The stage is yours, sweetie.

Danny chose a day soon after the hyacinths had opened, to come out to his parents. He thought his family would love him no matter what. He also knew he loved men no matter what. He figured if they didn't approve, he at least had the weather. Luckily, he got both the beautiful day *and* his parents. So when they opened their arms to him, he called the day "God throwing a party."

So what do you think?

Not bad. And that line about God's party. You don't forget a thing, Bicie. A guy's got to watch what he says around you. But I have to admit it was a good line, not, tal vez, *my most original line, but a good one.*

Yeah, Danny, and a real compliment coming from a guy who knew how to host the best kind. Remember what you used to say? *You have to plan a little, my Bicie.*

I became "Bicie" at seven and a half when Leah couldn't say "Beatrice." Sometimes I signed my name B.C. when I wrote Leah. Before Christ, of course. Before cocks, meaning sex, since that was her choice and mostly mine. Before California, that's where she and Eli moved after college. Before cracks, when we were just two sisters, not grown up, just kids, whole. Before childhood, when we lingered in our mother's womb, six years apart.

"You can't just invite your friends and hope for the best. What will you serve? How will you arrange it? I'm telling you, Beastie"–Danny's alternate invention–"you'll never catch a man with a table setting like that."

"And have I told you that I already have one man too many, present company excluded?"

"Why you left him I'll never understand. Cute, smart, a professor provider."

"And I don't have my *own* income?"

"A do-good lawyer. Come on, sweetie, you need a pension, a plan. You need a man."

"Danny, you just may find yourself off my party list."

But you couldn't give a party without him. Not just its life, he became every party's soul. The reason people stayed long past the time they told the babysitter they'd return. You couldn't pull away from him. That kind of person. That kind of friend.

When you visited him, you came home. You relaxed. You sat down on the floor, on the carpet so thick it seemed swollen, like a river, full of plump fish and dark stories at its bottom, but at the top, soft and light. You could float there, caressed by the sound of his voice and the way he had of making a joke out of anything.

Beastie, you make me uncomfortable. I feel like I shouldn't listen.

That's why I used the disguised voice again, so you could appreciate the story, not find fault, as you usually do. Let me continue. Back to Bicie basics, and no interruptions from you, okay?

Okay.

When I told you Michael would kill me if I came late to pick them up from Mitch's, remember your response? Classic Danny. *I'm getting you out to your car now, Beastie. I don't want you to die at the hands of your son. It would be both tragic and embarrassing.* You made me laugh when I felt like crying about how Michael had gotten so hostile that year. Michael got over it, just like you promised.

But Danny has not yet managed to find a way to settle the civil war between Leah and me. So, as always, he comes, now with Emma at his side, to help shore me up for Leah's Passover visit. My turn this year. We keep up the tradition. Even years in Chicago, odd years in Santa Monica. Leah and Eli's son Raoul would come from Oberlin. Randi would bring her new boyfriend, but Michael would come alone. His girlfriends he kept to himself, except for Monita, the one we met and wept about when they split up.

April 19, 2008. Passover changes every year, and this year it falls on the same night it fell sixty-five years ago, the night of the Warsaw Ghetto Uprising.

My sister's not the only one I struggle with. An old friend sends me her e-mail address. I don't reply, afraid we'd end up where we left off. Arguing about Israel. Salting wounds with bitter herbs. My sister, a few years ago, started to condemn Sharon. *Progress*, I think. And then I cringe. *At what cost?*

I learned to look for the good in people from my grandmother, the one who followed Emma Goldman everywhere she went. From my grandfather I learned to see through the good to the bad, or its potential. Immigration law, a perfect choice for me. I help good people get through a system set up by bad ones. Danny stopped me every time I talked like that. *It's not all one way or the other, Beastie. You think all the good ones line up over here, and the bad ones there? If only. Then we could shoot the ones over there. Oh, excuse me, I think that's been tried. Didn't work.*

I know he was attacking my tendency toward self-righteousness. Frankly, I'm really glad he came back so he could see that I've improved, made my own kind of progress. Matured. No one is all good or all bad. A simple truth that takes a lot of us a lifetime to get. The all or nothing thinkers. Gamblers, I guess you'd call us. Mood swingers. Bi-polars. Manic-depressives. I used to think everyone thought that way except for a very few actually cheerful people, cheerful by nature, not by medication, or meditation. They were just born that way. The kind who always say "good morning" when I'm still wondering how I ever made it out of bed. But there appear to be more of them than us. More than I would have thought growing up Jewish, and paranoid.

What I've learned, though, is that even cheerful people have moods, and even a mean thought or two. That's what I'm figuring out. Mitch is not a saint, after all. Thank God. It still doesn't mean I can go back to him. I know too much, or maybe not enough.

When people say things about someone like "he doesn't have a mean bone in his body," maybe they're really saying how much they love that person, or that they depend on that person to see them through. Or to remember them when they die. I don't know. Maybe I'm just too evil myself. Not evolved enough. Not big enough. But you know what I think? Not one of us escapes a mean bone or two.

Stop!

Danny came through pretty clear that afternoon of New Year's Eve, the day he came back to me. Mitch and I had just split up, and I knew the twins' birthday party would offer a challenge for all of us. I think the kids handled it better than I did. I kept thinking that I had made a mistake. Why had I left this great guy? Mitch was skinny and walked with a limp from the clubfoot surgeons mostly repaired years ago. He had allergies. He had problems with his back. *And* he was sexy and smart and never complained about anything. That was it. He never complained. He was always in a good mood. He loved everything I did. He supported my decision to go to law school when the twins started nursery school. Hell, he paid my tuition and cheered the loudest when I passed the bar. He put up with everything, my insecurities, my buried grief about my sister that had become an obsession, my fears that something would happen to the twins at the playground, during an overnight trip to a friend's house, or on a ride in the seat-belt broken neighbor's station wagon. Always St. Mitch would calm me, never become impatient, and hold me when I outlined all the bad things that could happen. But I knew that we couldn't go on like this. He had taken the place of my dead mother, and I was no longer twelve, or fifteen, or even nineteen. I needed to stand on my own, and that's the one thing Mitch wouldn't let me do. That's what I knew in my clear moments, but it took me a while to stop punishing myself for leaving the greatest husband on the block, and on really bad days, the greatest husband any woman has ever known. Do you see what I mean about my problem with gray areas?

So Danny plopped himself down in my head, not like my grandparents or my mother, not responding to questions I'd ask, pleas for guidance, but in the middle of my head, taking the initiative, announcing his arrival by reminding me that I needed to go easy on myself and give Mitch an inch or so as well.

I often wonder if I would have chosen Mitch if Mom had lived. They say girls who like boys look for their fathers when they want to marry, but I went after a mom substitute. Someone who would comfort me as Mom did that last summer. I forgot to mention our other "B.C." Before cancer. Her diagnosis came at the end of my sophomore year in high school, and just when she could see the remission medal and only had to reach maybe half a foot to get it, the disease grabbed her hand, pushed it back, and hope fell away forever. But that summer, that last summer, I sat with her every day, and we had those words, which, with a different kind of luck, could have spread out over thirty, or even maybe forty, years. I settled in with my mother, watching her watching me, keeping track of where I went off track and how long it took me to meander back. I understood a whole lot sooner that she wasn't really disappointed with my lack of ambition just frustrated by my second guessing myself every step of my way toward the future. And she promised me a future filled with love and *mazel*, which has more or less transpired except I can't sit with it. Worry and restlessness a more familiar friend to me than all other companions combined.

Dios mio! *This is why I came back, my* bubeleh.

I actually loved how Danny switched from Spanish to Yiddish, any means necessary to enhance his English.

You need to get yourself free. Stop with the hair shirt and on with the bustier. You need to figure out why you need to punish yourself. Of course, in a country taken over by Puritans, inhabited by their children along with a fair amount of Catholics and a critical mass of Jews, who would wonder? You've got just cause for worry, guilt, and grief.

Danny loved my mom like a second mother. He listened to all her stories and memorized the best of them. He borrowed from them, especially the sad ones about how her mother left her at the home for children, when she divorced my grandfather. My grandmother thought her two children—Rosie and Morrie—would keep each other from getting lonely.

Morrie, the brother Rosie adored, the one who taught her how to read way before kindergarten. He had started first grade and fell in love with phonics, so when they went to the silent movies together, he'd whisper the captions in her ear. One day, she said, "I want to do that." So Morrie took her home and sat her down and broke the code for her. The sounds and symbols that opened a world that did not shut down until she died. My mother became a reader; it kept her sane. Morrie, who bequeathed her a gift like no other, would have saved her from the loneliness of that place, that school, one step above an orphanage. What her immigrant mother could afford after she split from the husband whose cold and cruel reactions to life had wiped the world of all its color. But Morrie disappeared, leaving my mother only stories and the kind of memories a six-year-old girl can tend to. As Jack pulled Morrie's body from under the car that had run over him and carried his limp body up the stairs to their apartment, he broke into a howl that turned into the words my mother would never forget, *Why my Morrie? Why him? Why not you?*

His golden child gone, Jack thought he would follow Morrie to the grave. Instead he piled this, the worst of all his other pains and injuries, on top of his already broken spirit and hurled what hurt him at the one who stood sobbing at his side. My little mother.

I loved her for surviving it. For making almost all of the other childhood stories she told entrepreneurial or philosophical. Like how the kids at the home, mostly boys, would find parking spots for shoppers on crowded Saturdays and then ask for payment for their trouble. They knew the side streets that always had a spot or two. Then there was their scheme of making soap out of sand at the beach. Who knew what had entered their minds or what stray piece of science had built this illusion? And my mother's explanation for her father's unforgivable outburst, *He had his reasons. The Cossacks killed his father and raped his mother. His wife was leaving him. And now his only son lay limp in his arms.*

But I could not forgive him for hurting her like that. Danny thought I should show more sympathy for Jack and understanding for my mother.

Come on, Danny. She needed to get angry. The bastard hardly ever saw her, and then when he moved to Los Angeles, he promised her a new winter coat, something she hadn't had in years. Stylish, like she wanted. At thirteen, her looks started happening, and she knew clothes could make them work even harder for her. And the jerk reneged, pulled out, canceled one more promise.

Yeah, yeah. Not the best of dads, but he was her *dad.*

Leah never seemed to have the same concern about Jack. Maybe it's my first child sense of fairness and justice, or maybe it's that Mom would routinely tell me I looked like him. Oddly, I think she meant it as a compliment, but I never took it that way. Instead, it put me on a mission to disassociate myself from him by any means I could manage. He was cruel, so I'd be kind. He was adrift; I became persistent. He was unhappy; I worked at cheerful. Of course, I could handle kindness and persistence, but I never got the hang of good spiritedness. It came out forced, phony. Full of tortured anxiety, my good moods frightened most people I tried them on. Danny saw right through the act and loved the failed actor. He had no time for my anti-Jack persona, fragile or otherwise.

Leah, as a child, came to sunny moods without any effort, but she's been a grown up now for thirty years or more, depending on how you count them. So I must remind myself that although still my sister, she is no baby. A babe, and a brainy one at that, but no little sister. And along the way she took a turn no one would have guessed. We performed a kind of reversal. As her goal setting waned, mine advanced. As I learned to balance my ups and downs, she became more melancholic.

Straight out of the honors program at the University of Michigan, Leah and Eli went off to California to earn a pair of doctorates at UCLA; Leah, in English and Eli, in political science. She acquired hers in less than five years and wrote a stunning, breath-taking, ground-breaking–you get the idea–dissertation on Emily Dickinson's use of architectural elements in her investigation of death and sorrow called "'A Swelling of the Ground': Emily Dickinson's Shelter, Sorrow, and Prosody." Then she quit. She quit Westwood Village where she and Eli had established themselves in a large apartment entertaining fellow grad students; she quit writing poetry; she quit reading; she tried to quit Eli, but he proved more successful than Mitch in holding on to his run-away Rubenstein girl. Then, she became pregnant and started going to flea markets, using a search for baby clothes as her alibi. Unconvinced, Eli kept quiet so she'd come home. He learned to dance with Leah and didn't mind that she moved him around one floor after the other always taking the lead and sealing his defeat. You could call it that, or you could call it his happiness.

After nine years in grad school, teaching part-time at Santa Monica College, Eli finally managed to get his Ph.D., but now damaged goods–failure to progress in good time–

he could only get a tenure track position at a community college or state university. Content to stay put, he hired on at the college full-time where he realized he preferred the mostly working class students, getting their family's first whiff of a college education, over the upper middle class kids he taught as a lecturer at UCLA. His own parents had sacrificed everything so that he could go to Michigan, and he knew that even a community college education meant a sacrifice for the parents of a fair number of his students. He remembered my mother's stories about Chicago's Crane College, called then, for better or worse, a "junior college." She dreamt about going to the University of Chicago or at least down state, the University of Illinois at Urbana-Champaign, but she knew only Crane fit into her mother's budget. In fact, the hours she attended classes took away from what she could contribute to the bills at home, where she had returned for good at age thirteen, the year of the promised and never delivered winter coat. Anyway, she thrived at Crane where she read Cervantes in Spanish, acted in school theater productions, and debated politics with her classmates and professors. So Eli never saw his job as a defeat; in his mind, he paid back what my mother had received, which had vicariously enriched him.

Meanwhile, Leah grew more serious about flea markets. She roamed for the first few months, talking to people, getting a sense of prices and bargaining rules. She watched for the regulars and saw how they handled professional dealers. She decided she'd specialize in silver and then started falling back to the next rung of the market: garage and estate sales.

She bought up old silver wherever she could find it and then sold it to dealers for a profit, sometimes at a stall at the market that she began to rent on a regular basis and sometimes to their shops. She'd look for candlestick holders that had become separated from their mates, which reduced their value to the average customer. Like an eager child given the gift of toys a parent had promised for a long time and had finally purchased, she came home with her stash. Then, while Raoul took his nap, she sat hammering away on the backyard patio of the bungalow, the place she and Eli bought in Santa Monica with their little red coppers, the bungalow that would later alchemy into its own precious bundle. She pounded open the candlestick holders in order to remove the non-silver materials, the cement used to keep all the parts together. Then she sold the silver to dealers for a profit and went back for more.

In her own way my sister found the peace she needed, and she discovered that the hunt for silver, and other items which she decided to specialize in, resembled the scholar's quest for one more obscure article or rare book that would feed an argument. For example, she started collecting old fraternity pins. Not sure why at first, but like the academic working off a hunch, she knew she might be on to something. Besides, she appreciated the cultural artifact they represented. They popped up a lot in the seventies when the Greek system took a downswing for a while, along with white weddings. Then in the eighties, when the Greeks and the weddings and movies without a social conscience returned, she discovered a market for old fraternity pins. Fraternity brothers, nostalgic for their college years and appalled that their pins floated around garage sales and flea markets, spent money to get them out of circulation.

So, you could say, my sister experienced a mild, unnoticed nervous breakdown, a delayed reaction to my mother's death and a more immediate reaction to moving through Dickinson's morbid jewels. From the ashes of those reactions, she eventually made a minor mint.

What does a person have to do to break into this conversation?

That was Emma. It concerned her, of course, that Leah had gone so far from our grandmother's beliefs. I never got the whole story, but I did know that after Ida left Jack, she met Abe. A match made not in heaven but in the hope for it. Anarchist meetings and speeches and books. Together they fell in love with Emma Goldman and then with each other.

I'm proud to say I started more than a few successful unions. It's part of what we struggled for. Free love. The kind that grew out of a similar way of believing and acting and dreaming. We had our dreams. We had our work. People like your Ida and Abe understood. They believed in the good of the common person and the promises we could make to each other without need for any government taking up our cause. Only we knew what we needed and how it would go. Maybe not a direct line from here to there. It would meander. It would grow. It would blossom. In the hands of youth and others who knew that you get to "there" from believing in the process that starts "here." Too many plans only build prisons, and prisons don't work. We need to tear them down and build places of rejuvenation.

And religion? Nationalism? How did your sister move so far away from our dreams?

Even though lawyers don't usually look at meandering as a way to victory, I loved Emma because she represented a way back to our grandparents, Ida and Abe. Jack, I left to rot. Oh, I shouldn't put it that way. But since he showed no interest in us, I never bothered with him. Maybe if Mom had given him a grandson, he'd have visited, but I think he figured neither of us could bring his Morrie back. That's what he lived for, and when he saw that his own actual son given to him by his second wife would never substitute for Morrie, he sank, along with the stone he hung around his neck the day Morrie died. But Ida found Emma, and Abe, so she could breathe again, never the same full breath like before the loss that broke her in half, but in a way that prepared her for the war and the other losses, the private holocaust that bled public.

Little did I know that the other Rubenstein sister had become as fixed to holocaust history, past and present, as I did. I thought I alone carried that depressive gene, that saturnine legacy from Jack. Sunny Leah, though, found her way to it. Perhaps Dickinson led her there. The WASP girl who dwelled in an exquisite exile of her own making. Leah's "Never Again!" followed more traditional lines. Her call for security clashed with my cry for integrity. The heartbreak? That one seemed to cancel the other–our own stone. The stone we brought each year as we gathered at the table for the family Seder under the constant blue skies of Santa Monica or the grayer ones of Chicago's often tepid start into spring. Of *course,* you say, a Jew obsessed with security would hold holocaust history close to her breast. Yes. Now I know about the journals, how at first Leah carried the satchel with her on planes and trains and long car trips, any time she left home for more than a few days. That's how Eli described it. A satchel.

"Probably from Abe, don't you think?"

"Dad gave all that stuff away."

"Bicie, you think your sister didn't know how to hide treasures. Now she digs them up. Before, she buried them. I think she hid that satchel underneath her old bed."

"So that's why she wouldn't let Dad sweep. He would have thrown that thing out."

"It remained empty for many years. Just waiting. And then she filled it up."

I didn't know how to handle this. The way Eli told it, Leah barely balanced on some frightening ledge of her own construction.

Don't worry so much, mi Beastie. My plan unfolds. This trial together with Leah this year will give you strength, journals or not. What you never knew you knew. Just like how you nursed Paloma, mi hermana, my sweetness.

Danny and I became friends in eighth grade, and his baby sister Paloma brought us together. He and I had known each other's name and face from across the crowded room of forty-three kids stashed into a classroom that could never have predicted the baby boom but ended up accommodating it better than most people would have expected. Of course, we had to go on double shifts to make it work. One group from eight to noon, and the other from noon to four. No one could have imagined all the sex that the ending of a war like World War II can instigate. The war after the one that promised to end all of them, the war that broke open into camps and poured breathing bones into the arms of innocent soldiers. They had killed as soldiers do, and they had seen their friends blow apart as soldiers do, but they had never seen bones like this, or carried them out of their graves. This, soldiers had not done before, so when they came home, they wanted alcohol and cigarettes, and they wanted sex. Liquor stores boomed; tobacco companies grew; schools expanded.

And into our school the four Gonzalez kids arrived–Paloma in first grade; Cecilia in third grade; Abelardo in seventh; Danny in eighth. The four of them comprised the entire Mexican American population at Benjamin Franklin Elementary School. The rest of us, all white, were about half Jewish and half not: Irish, WASP, Polish. Danny's father had determined that his kids would live in a new house across the viaduct from the South Chicago neighborhood, one of the neighborhoods in the city where Mexican Americans had settled into by the 50s. So Danny became my classmate, and Paloma became my charge.

Eighth graders had strict responsibilities. We served as patrol guards, recess monitors, and room captains. When Mrs. Martin announced my name for room captain of first grade, Room 111, I celebrated my luck. A prized job, it meant I got to leave class early for recess and early for going home, because I had to go down the three flights of stairs from Room 305 to 111, so I could help the first graders get on their hats, coats, and boots in the winter and line up straight in the fall and the spring, leading them quietly and orderly out of the building. My job, easily justified in the cold months, continued during the less obviously challenging ones. If anyone had questioned why no seasonal lay-offs, I would have argued that the first graders depended on my ability to keep them from getting distracted by the burning leaves in the fall and the blooming flowers in the spring. The outdoors should not become an issue until all the indoor matters had finished. And Paloma, always ready to climb outside, pulled on me as we headed out the door to recess or home. I still remember how her little hand hugged mine. It felt like heaven. At the end of the day, Danny gathered his three younger siblings–Paloma, Cecilia, and Abelardo–and led them all home. Then, I'd go find my friends, Andrea and Cheryl, for the slog back to our own block. Leah, one year older than Paloma and our collective little sister, since Andrea and Cheryl's older siblings had long ago abandoned them, waited eagerly as I passed Paloma to Danny and took my own sister's dear little seven-year-old hand into mine. In those days Leah looked upon Paloma as one more sister, along with Andrea and Cheryl, but this one, this beautiful little girl with thick, straight dark hair and brown eyes, like Leah's, and not much younger than Leah became the baby sister Leah secretly longed for, she told me years later, so she could finally change her status to "big and in charge."

"I pretended she was mine, Bicie. She looked more like me than you did, with your red curls and hazel eyes. My little sister. *Bonita*, her brother always called her. I made up stories about how I would save her when she got sick."

First, Paloma missed a few days here and there, and then she missed six weeks. When she returned, her face had turned puffy with the medication they said would help her fight the leukemia but may have killed her sooner than the disease would have. I thought I'd break in two when her teacher told me she had died. I didn't know what to say when I saw Danny, so I just told him how Paloma would always talk about him as she clasped my hand on the way out of Benjamin Franklin twice a day.

"She talked about me?"

"Oh, yeah, all the time," I exaggerated.

"What did she say?"

"That you taught her how to tie her shoelaces and that you helped her on with her boots and that you showed her how to fold her paper straight so she could write her addition facts in a neat column and that you let her read out loud to you and..."

"She said all that?"

"And more."

I started up again, but Danny brushed his index finger back and forth across his mouth to silence me. So I learned how memories could hurt, but later I figured out that if you push them away, they crawl under your skin and pop up in unexpected places and stubborn ways. They have their *movidas* all right.

Take Danny's comic act. His memories walked right in and sat just off to the side while he ridiculed the nuns at Our Lady Crown of Heaven, who told him Paloma went with God to a better place. He didn't talk about Paloma or how the nuns promised salvation of her soul. He just whipped out serious satire about the Catholic Church and dug in at the nuns, and people loved it. With more than half of the city Catholic–Irish, Polish, Mexican, Puerto Rican, Italian–they could relate. But I knew he didn't hate those nuns with their sometimes cruel and sometimes foolish ways. He hated that Paloma had died, and he had to find someone to blame. Some hold organized religion accountable for our need to blame, find fault, accuse, transfer responsibility, not step up to the plate, point the finger at someone else, and at the same time punish ourselves for the sins of living, breathing, cracking jokes, and making love. That would be my father in me talking. He had no use for any of it. Not exactly an atheist, as in my "atheist, anarchist, Jewish grandparents," Ida and Abe, closer to an agnostic, the uncertainty more intellectual, less political. My father called himself a secular Jew. Not lapsed–that implies devout at one time–but a status, a choice. You don't have to believe in God to be a Jew. You just need a Jewish mother.

So Danny would make fun of the nuns and the priests. He'd bite into them, shred them, core them, eviscerate them in a gentle teasing sort of way, which made his skewering even more delicious. But when he got sick, something changed. He told me he started loving the nuns, even the cruel ones. The pompous ones. The sadistic ones. The ones who played at humble to cover smug. The ones who called AIDS God's punishment for his sleeping with men.

"You're just afraid there's a hell and you're going to it."

"No, Beastie, I'm not afraid of those old nuns or anything else. Nothing but myself."

Then I heard his new bit. The one he based on my mother and one of the stories she told about a new dress and a teacher as mean as any of the nuns Danny used to roast. And I knew what he meant.

"This next one's about an old friend of mine, a lady called Rose. Now for starters, Rose is quite a name. Think of all its namesakes: rose quartz and rose candles, rose water and rosewood, rose windows and rose colored glasses, rose fever and Rose Cleaver—you didn't know June had a sister, well let me tell you...anyway, there's Rose of Sharon and Rose of Hollywood, quite a looker in *her* day. Then there's Rose of Maxwell Street, Santa Rosa, and my cousin Rosa. The rosaries of my childhood. The Rosetta Stone. Rosita Sanchez and Rosario Valdez. Rose Green. Rose Brown. Rose Clay. And little Rosie Kleinbaum, who had a mean teacher. Any of you out there ever have a teacher you didn't like, one you'd like to marinate maybe? Well, Rosie did. This little kid came from a poor family, a broken family, and in first grade, when they had it the worst, she had only one dress, which she had to wear everyday. Every night she would scrub it out and hang it up to dry, and then every morning, her mother would iron it, and Rosie would trudge off to school. Kind of like heading out to meet the wicked wolf in the forest. Little Red Riding Rose.

"So one day after Rosie's mother had saved enough of the pennies she earned working in retail for little commission and lots of confessions—you think those priests hear the good stuff, you oughta work lingerie for a day. *This one's for my mistress, and that one's for my wife who is pretty sure I have a mistress but will reconsider when I bring home a 'little something' for her, doncha think, lady? Whadya think, lady? Come on, I need a lady's opinion.* True to her daughter's name, Mrs. Kleinbaum blushed a little, the effect the...er...gentleman was looking for, and he bought both items, sure of himself and free of his guilt. Anyway, one day, with her hard earned pennies, Rosie's mother bought Rosie a new dress. It was a perfect dress, a creamy green for spring, fresh and clean. It smelled new. It looked new. And it felt new on Rosie's soft six-year-old skin. She couldn't wait to go to school the next day. She walked into class proud of her new dress, praying everyone would notice, and then she learned a lesson about the ways you don't want to be noticed."

At this point, some people in the audience started to squirm, wondering when the punch line would hit, but Danny didn't even notice. He just carried on.

"'Well, look at that, everyone! Rosie's got a new dress.' And as the teacher spoke in the phoniest sweet voice she could manage without making even herself feel bad, everyone looked and stared and remembered that Rosie hadn't had a new dress all year. Some of the kids started to laugh, the teacher's intended effect. Some of the boys thought Rosie looked pretty, and the girls *knew* she did. A few of them felt sorry for Rosie. But none of them said anything. If you said something, Miss O'Brien could take away your recess, send you to the principal, or maybe assign you a demerit for discourteous behavior. But Rosie had guts. She had *chutzpah*. She had *cajones*.

"She stood up and in the strongest voice she could manage without making even herself afraid she said, 'Miss O'Brien, you can take away my recess, but you can't take away my dress.' Now everyone in the class sat still, looking straight ahead, studying O'Brien's face, with its dull eyes and its smug nose and its tight mouth, to see where it would go next. Flustered, of course, but amazed at the courage of the little rebel, she carefully composed her answer. 'All right, Rose, you may sit down now. I won't take away your recess, and I won't take away your dress. Please sit down, Rose, and never, ever talk back to me again.'

"So what's the moral of this story? Well, I could say 'some days the wolf gets you, and some days you get the wolf,' but instead of a moral, I'm pitching more of a curve ball. You think O'Brien is the bad guy. She has all the makings. She's old, probably way out of shape. I already described her pitiful face. And all of that lets you let her be the monster. So she's the wolf, right? Wrong. The wolf is *you*. For hating her so much. And for all these years, too. Get over it. Miss O'Brien is only a stand in for the wolf. Mean? Cruel? Sure. She misused and abused her power. But you're not six years old anymore. Picking on that teacher is gonna get you nowhere. She was sad. She was miserable. She was wrong. But hating her doesn't make you right. It makes you hateful. Think about it. Besides, Rosie already gave her what for. And who knows what turned that teacher into the little torturer she had become? We all have our stories.

"So now I want you to close your eyes and picture that teacher you wanted to marinate a few minutes ago. I know we all have them. I've got more than one. You think a gay Mexican kid had it easy in public schools run by Irish Catholics who took more direction from the Pope than the school superintendent? No? *Bueno, mis chicos.* Now I want you to tell that teacher everything you wanted to but didn't have the guts to when you were six or ten, eleven, whatever. And then walk the hell away and pray for that teacher's soul. Get down on your Irish Catholic, German

Protestant, Polish Jewish, Pakistani Muslim, Chinese Buddhist, devout Hindu knees–even if your particular religion does not go on bended knee, just humor me for a minute. It's a metaphor, okay? So get down on your bent and pre-arthritic knees, and pray. After all, this scene takes place all in your mind, so no one's gonna feel any *real* pain. No physical pain, at least. Pray for that teacher and the wolf in you, and the wolf in her. And pray for recess. And pray for excess. And pray for whatever you need in your own goddamn life. And pray for me because I've got a year to live, or less. And I swear I'm not gonna go to my grave hating my grammar school teacher or hating myself. Amen."

People didn't know what to make of it. They had expected him to tear into that teacher, and when he didn't, they thought for a few seconds, time enough to feel ripped off at not getting their lick from the lion. They readjusted themselves in their seats. A couple of them coughed; a few cleared their throats. And then one of the guys, a beefy Chicago kinda guy, stood up and started clapping loudly and slowly. Others got up and joined him, women mostly, and then the men beside them. And then the men with men. And a dyke whistled. I think she started to get up on her chair but decided to limit the attention for one night. They didn't feel sorry for Danny. They were giving thanks. Like church or something, the real thing, what my father scoffed at because he never understood it even though my mother's measure of it drew him to her. That connection, that ability to dig up what buries us most, and sanctify it, say it. Danny left me with all of that before he died, and then he told me to go to Israel, to face the wolf of my own creation. You can bet Emma had a lot to say about that.

So Herzl won after all, it seems. Or maybe Hitler. Sacrilegious, you think, to speak of the Zionist leader in the same breath as the fuehrer? And what am I, Emma Goldman, if not sacrilegious? Religion. Government. Marriage. All prisons, big and small. And Israel? Jews safe and secure behind bars. So I certainly did not go along with Danny's travel plans for you, not that he consulted with me. "Go to Israel," Danny told you. "Go to hell!" I replied. But then I relented. I, who knew you cannot get to any where with a full-fledged plan from any here; I, who knew you had to wander a bit; I decided I'd put my trust in Danny's scheme, not faith, trust.

Danny brought Emma to me after Leah and I had our first fight over Israel. He brought her for support but also because he thought he could transform the two of us birds with one trip. I guess he knew that I'd have to be prepared for what Leah had secretly, off and on, been preparing for a long time.

Death is not good for nothing, Beastie.

JOURNALS: 1

Do you think we should tell her?

What and worry her more? My Beastie, your Beatrice, Leah's B.C. does not need to know now that the crisis has passed.

How can we know that for sure?

Leah has stabilized. She is back to writing in her journals. As long as she keeps up that project, she can manage.

But, Gonzalez, this is not a healthy way to live.

And you think we're the best to advise on this matter?

Well, of course, I'm not referring to our present state. Why would someone like Beatrice put so much confidence in us if we didn't have a thing or two to say about survival?

I think Eli can handle it. He knows Leah better than anyone. He's monitoring the journals.

Sweet boy, that one. He knows when to interfere. A good boy.

I agree. He decided it did not detract from his natural honesty, integrity, and inborn virtue. This is the equivalent of a lie of omission. Less high up on the bad deed scale. In fact, when it has been determined that you did it to save someone's life or sanity or any other aspect of their well-being, you get a waiver.

Yes, well, you know about those things. Being an atheist, I don't participate.

Mi abuelita, lapsed Catholics, excommunicated Catholics, Catholics who haven't been to confession for years, dead

31

Catholics who can't remember the last time they went to church, we congregate and consult all the good and holy books and any former followers and laws of the righteous, and then we decide what's what. All honest atheists are welcome. You could call it a rite of the unorganized. A religion made in heaven—if you'll pardon the double take—for anarchists.

Okay, Gonzalez, okay. So you think Eli knew about that night?

He knew.

How do you know he knew?

Because he followed her to the motel.

To the motel? What motel, Gonzalez?

The one she went to so she could do herself in.

How can you be so calm? And how did he follow her?

In his car, Emma. How else do you follow anyone in Los Angeles?

How did he manage to keep her from knowing?

You think that Leah in this kind of state or any other kind of state, actually, pays much attention to traffic, except to stay out of accidents? Listen, Emma, he even got a room right next to hers. And while she contemplated this or that other method, he concentrated on all the sounds. Toilet flushing, throat clearing, sobbing.

And what was his plan?

His plan was that if it got quiet for too long, he'd start pounding on the door and then on the window. He figured he'd know how long was too long. Good instincts.

And then?

And, then, Emma, just when he started to get up to activate his system, he heard her drop her keys on the floor and go to the door.

Because she had decided to stay put and return home?

Yes, she knew she could not do this to him or Raoul, but it was a wrestling match, an indoors, interior space, bloody brained wrestling match. She came close, and so did Eli.

To what, Gonzalez?

To charging in on her.

Gonzalez, there is something not quite right about this story. It's hard to believe. I mean, I can't exactly visualize it. The two motel rooms, the thin walled sound monitoring program, the risk that she hadn't brought a gun that she could have used in the middle of the sobbing. I just don't buy it.

Well, mi abuelita, your detective instincts remain intact, it didn't exactly happen that way. I was just painting a kind of picture of the relationship between Leah and her devoted, beloved husband. Synchronized, trusting, psychologically interwoven. Physically inseparable.

*So what **really** happened that night, Gonzalez?*

What really happened I can't say in so many words. Leah came close to killing herself, and Eli entered her dreams while she slept and saved her, over and over and over again. By the time she woke up, though she remembered none of it, after he left to teach his classes in the morning and she dropped off Raoul at school, she pulled out her journal and started writing again.

Thank God.

I thought you didn't believe.

An expression, Gonzalez, an expression.

And so Eli read what Leah wrote that morning.

Where is it written or allowed that we can commit such crimes? Is it a synapse that got stuck at hate, or does evil keep its own realm taunting us with a simple walk across a narrow bridge? How did we forget that the inferno always lies in wait? That none of us is holier than its grab for our honor and our pain. What is the reason for our brain wanting that leap into the fire, thinking somehow it will not leave a mark?

Even if we manage to make our way over without falling into the pit below, we should go through some kind of ritual cleansing, so the evil does not dig into our skin and soul, burrowing there for protection, like some parasite that can't survive without its host.

I thought my people were the holy ones. The ones with reason, who had risen from their injuries to walk along the side of the just, to never abandon the needy. But which people did not think this about their own people? Which of their holy books did not sanctify this desperate need to defend the weak against the disorder of the cruel? Any people, even my people, I now believe, can become corrupt and suck the sweet flesh from a child. And, if not fallen, if somehow balanced, precarious on that rope across the hole, how to remember no one is free from falling off into the place of wretched horror?

Oi, Gonzalez! She needs some help. She needs some grounding. She needs to get back to a flea market or two and sell her wares.

She will, Emma. She also needs these moments. She's moving toward something, a place where she might get some rest.

Rest, I'm afraid, may do her in. She needs to keep moving and not wallow. This is not a healthy direction. Like the other sister, too much obsession.

I'm not sure of that, Emma. I think this can help her.

Well, maybe if she had a friend or two to talk with about her mishegoss, *someone who could keep her from the center of this ever raveling spool.*

Who? Eli? Beastie? She's afraid to let them in. Her friend Rhoda doesn't understand. Raoul could handle it, but he's not old enough yet. She's going to have to manage on her own for a while.

I just hope she can make it through. If something happens to her, we lose Beatrice, too.

I know this, Emma. Don't you realize that's why I dragged you here?

THE ERNEST BIRNBAUM MEMORIAL CLUB

After going together for five years, my parents married in 1937, in September. My dad's best friend, Ernie, the boyfriend of my mom's best friend, Sylvia, had introduced them to each other. But after Sylvia broke Ernie's heart, he joined the Communist Party, went to Spain with the Abraham Lincoln Brigade and didn't come back. My dad felt guilty, like he should have gone with Ernie, even though to him the Party represented one more religion, one more way of taking orders from the colonel, the priest, the commander. The cause, he believed in, but he believed in my mother more, and stayed. I'm grateful. Lots of those guys didn't make it back.

So after they got word that Ernie died, they and their friends, including Ernie's sister Shirley and her husband Hank, set up The Ernest Birnbaum Memorial Club. They raised money and sent it to the Abraham Lincoln Brigade for guns and medicine. But underfunded, ill-trained, up against the fascists without any backing from the so-called allies, the international brigades failed. And Franco, making deals with the devil, set up shop for years. By the time Hitler invaded Poland, a few weeks before my parents' second anniversary, World War II crept closer to its own done deal.

Older than the parents of my friends, Dad didn't get called to serve after Pearl Harbor. Instead, he taught high school history and explained the war and its root causes to his students, many of whom did serve. He persuaded some from quitting school and signing up. After graduation, when most of the guys told him they had closed their own private deals with the war, he did not try to dissuade them. Not a pacifist, he knew this war had just cause, but he also knew how part of him got blown up in Spain along with Ernie.

From 1942 until 1946, my mother tried to get pregnant. She succeeded four times, but only I arrived, in 1947. All the other girls would have been Elizabeth Michelle; the boys, Bernard Morris, after my mother's Aunt Bessie and her brother Morrie. For me she decided to change her luck. I became Beatrice Marilyn. Two muses. One ancient and known, the other modern and not yet a legend. You'd think I'd have inherited my mother's movie-star-in-a-Jewish-girl-sort-of-way looks because they, too, inspired, although on a lesser plane. Instead, I came out with a nose that already looked too big, even on a baby. Still, the relatives called me *shayna punim*, pretty face.

Danny always hated it when I put down my looks, but just when I started to feel that I could at least call myself appealing, one of my high school friends would shove a make-up magazine in my face.

"There is no reason nowadays for a woman to look unattractive."

I knew that meant a session would show its own unattractive presence before too long, a make-up session, where my friends would meet and, say, match me up with the correct eye shadow color, show me how to apply just the right amount of eye liner so I wouldn't look fast like Cindy Schwartz, and present me with my own eyelash curler when they finished. When I appeared in school the next day with more eye shadow on one eye than the other, they told me I should just stick to blush, that, in a pinch, my eyes could stand on their own. But I could never remember where to apply. I think the hollow below my cheekbone promised to make my nose look smaller, but the girls had advised me that I could address the circles under my eyes—from staying up too late reading—with the blush on the bones themselves. So I had a decision to make: big nose or eye bags? I alternated, figuring each day I wouldn't look half-bad, or actually, *only* half-bad. The summer before sophomore year, the real Marilyn killed herself, so I rested my case about how looks can't save your life.

Tallish with modest hips and no breasts to speak of or to stare at, my body disappointed my girlfriends even further, because they really did love me and worried that I had little hope for success in the necessary-looks department to capture the necessary-man component. They didn't know what to do with me except to recommend padded bras and flats. Later I saw that lovers and babies did just fine with my breasts. As for the lack of hips, I will argue that certain styles and looks return, making vintage stores popular and women like me, and the flappers, pretty cool from time to time.

I loved my girls, Andrea and Cheryl, but now with our old grammar school days behind us, they had started to get on my nerves. Around a different bend I saw a few underground types who wore black a lot and seemed to *emphasize* the dark circles under *their* eyes. Linda Newman and Lisa Gottlieb. They belonged to the Student Peace Union and hung out with guys from the University of Chicago. Seemed pretty romantic to me, both politically and erotically.

"College boys? Please, Bicie. It's too soon."

Alarmed that I would grow up too fast, my mother kept me close to her. I envied Leah in a perverse kind of way. With Mom gone when she started high school, she operated as a free agent.

So, Danny's little Beastie, your mother's death helped your sister gain her independence. Something the middle class women in my youth and in yours made big noises about, but refused to pay the price for. A small price, really. No price, actually. Sexual liberation for the loss of male protection. Who wants protection? You can't have it both ways anyway, but some of you thought so. Of course, I have a heart. I'm sorry your mother died so young, but these things happen. You make the best of them.

Sometimes Emma just had regular conversations with me instead of speechifying.

Young lady, if not for my speeches, Ida and Abe and a whole generation of men and women would not have progressed. You think you came so far, well, who helped you get there?

Emma, you know I'm grateful. Why do you think I brought you back from college for Leah?

I sometimes wonder, Beatrice. It seems the older sister meant to teach the younger, but perhaps Leah ended up learning more than you.

She's a Zionist, Emma, a nationalist.

And, so you think that just because she went astray, she lost the cause? Look, sweetie, Gonzalez has been working on me, too. You need to examine the situation further. Think about it this way. We did not approve of communism and its never withering state, but we thanked the idealistic ones, like your Uncle Ernie, for trying to save the Republic in Spain, for working in good faith with the anarchists. We didn't believe in conscription, but fighting for the cause? A wholly different matter. Sixty-seven years old, Berkman gone, I went to Spain. I would not denounce the anarchists who made league with the communists even though I'd already seen what they gave us. My disillusionment with Russia, and all of that. But we all became desperate about Spain.

And then she sighed a long sigh full of grief perhaps only a ghost has time for; the rest of us, still too busy trying to survive.

Okay, Beatrice, back to your sister. You need to see how she got to where she sits now. You need not to condemn. You need more compassion. And more sex.

Emma. I don't need you prying everywhere.

Prying? Danny tells me you have a good man. Devoted. All the right things. Good politics. Good in bed. You think I think you should marry him again? Of course not. But a coalition might work.

When Emma moved around like this, from Leah to Spain to Mitch, I got a little dizzy. But I knew she had her point. She lived the personal of the political. I didn't mind her jumping from here to there. After all, if I wanted coherence, I could read her essays. Clear, focused, persuasive. No wonder Ida and Abe signed on.

You don't sign on to anarchism. You live it. You eat it like a thick roast beef sandwich dressed with the best horseradish in town. You relish it. Like poetry.

I can't even have a private thought without Emma getting a whiff of it. I think she's programmed to tune in for words like "political" and names like "Ida and Abe."

Yes, dear, you could also use a little poetry in your life.

I tried, Emma. Danny thought I sounded weird.

Well, then, what about theater? The great American theater came after I died, as I predicted it would. O'Neill we already had, but then came Williams, Miller, Hellman—another not so nice Jewish girl. Hansberry—such a pity for brilliance to die so young, and this August Wilson. He roamed the century, gave it hell. And let's not forget the new Jewish kid. The Kushner. What an imagination that one's got, turning commentary into poetry.

I started to feel like I had walked into one of Emma's lectures. She must have sensed my impatience, not that I didn't find her ability to keep up fascinating, I just needed to get some work done, or something.

Get out of the house, Beatrice. Stop feeling so sorry for yourself. Go to a play.

Emma knew I worked too much, so on days like this she wins halfway. I don't necessarily plop down with *Angels in America*, but I give up my work plans and drive out to Waldheim Cemetery where they buried her near the Haymarket Monument, what started the struggle for her, in 1886 in my hometown. Alive, she could not live here; dead, she could rest. I love Chicago. I love the drive to the cemetery through the old West Side neighborhoods, and the quiet there. The muggy summer morning feels like family. What you come back to. What you know. Frozen icicles on your ears in the winter. Then, too hot for most and just right for me in July, even August. And the love notes of spring and fall. The wonder that anything could come to color again after winter, and that air could cool after hothouse summer. Family, cousins, old friends, who save your life when you need them, these days, this weather. Familiar. I *know* you. I *love* you. I will never forget you. How could Leah leave all this for the perfect climate of the angels in their everlasting heaven by the sea?

I wonder what Emma would think about my poetic twists and turns, my weak attempts to be more Leah-like, but she doesn't speak when I go to Waldheim. She goes on strike. She refuses her icon status. She refuses worship of any kind. But today when I make the trip just before Leah and Eli's arrival, she decides to break that routine. Even she acknowledges the importance of the next week and figures I need some extra guidance.

You want to know why I don't talk here, Beatrice. I don't like these statues to heroes. Those people who shine and sparkle get all the attention. And the credit. In my younger days, I derived great pleasure from that status, but I sobered up at the end. I learned the way of legends. Writers of history gather up all the good and brave deeds and bundle them in one package, making distribution easier. Then, all the plain and ordinaries, like Ida and Abe, for a couple of examples, get cheated out of their just glory. Later, after I died, they invented television, a foolish past time with programs like 'Queen for a Day', and your generation had this Andy Warhol fellow—trying to reduce fame from twenty-four hours to fifteen minutes. Well, there's a lot more shining in each and every life, but you'd never know it if you pick up a newspaper, turn to your favorite channel, walk those gold stars of Hollywood Boulevard. The real legends? The real history makers? Your grandparents, their friends. You, even. The never to be rich or famous. But happy perhaps. Maybe not. Maybe too much tragedy in the world. Fulfilled, then. That kind of golden. That kind of life.

Emma, this feels like a one-sided conversation. How do you want me to respond? I came here for strength, and you give me grief.

The appropriate response at a cemetery.

Emma, you know what I meant.

Look. I appreciate that young people have not forgotten me. I appear in novels, a Broadway musical, a simpering PBS special, and, gratefully, in that play I'd like you to read. But the matter with all of that, including this very piece of fantasy in which we participate right now, becomes my issue. Go live your own life. Stop whimpering at the gravesites of so-called heroes of history. Go make your own.

On my way home from the cemetery, I stop off at a deli that has survived the Jewish move to the suburbs and buy myself a bismarck, like Abe used to bring us on Sunday mornings, along with shrimp, barbecued in a little shack near the Calumet River, and smoked fish. I raise my coffee cup in a mock toast to him and Ida. Luckily no one notices my mime. Then I order a roast beef sandwich–extra on the horseradish–to go, for Emma.

Whatever Emma says about herself and heroism, she can't deny she dug out a groove in the road, and I'm glad

Ida and Abe followed it. I'm glad they trotted after her and tamed her for me. Not that anyone could ever tame Emma, but they taught me to listen to what she had to say, so it would come back to me when the kids I hung out with in college fell in love with her, and with each other. Like Mitch and me.

One Saturday morning, early in our relationship, when the cold of early winter pushed its way through the charms of a late fall—not exactly the "damp, drizzly November of the soul," but qualifying for a reason to assess one's current relationship to mood and melancholia—Mitch said he wanted to tell me a story, but first he needed to wash my feet.

"Like Jesus?"

"No, like the woman I love and never want to leave."

I caught that throw away as he pushed himself out from under our warm covers onto the cold floor of our minimally heated apartment. Before I could explain to him that long-term commitments were for people who hadn't lost their mother way too soon and so vowed to never love that hard again, Mitch had transported me from my undergraduate musings of Melville, Freud, and Jesus to his much more mature set of plans.

He went to his closet and pulled out an old porcelain basin that he later told me he had rescued from one of his mother's give away piles. Then he crossed the hall to the bathroom and filled it with warm water and enough drops of Dr. Bronner's liquid soap to create a sudsy oceanic antidote to the kind of low-level seasonal depression that afflicted me, not enough to launch a novel, more of a minor aggravation for which my beloved Mitch had just the cure. Anyway, almond was Mitch's favorite Dr. Bronner. It still is. How do I know? Well, when your ex-husband is an occasional lover, since your current lover doesn't mind, you shower at his house once in a while. You use the soap to wash yourself that he used all those years ago to seduce you. Not the first time, but around that first time.

So, after he gently pulled me into a sitting position along the side of the bed and put both my feet into the basin, he began to wash them with his hands, taking particular care with the places between my toes. It went on almost until I could no longer bear all of the attention, but he stopped just in time. He dried them, first my feet and then his hands, with a towel still slightly warm from the laundry he had gotten up early to fold, a gift from the days when guys could still hook us by cooking a meal, washing the dishes, and actually folding baskets of clean laundry. Now, ungrateful sensible women that we've become, we expect it.

What came next became the part I left out when I told Andrea and Cheryl about the foot bathing. Some things stay private. No one knows, except people poking their noses into novels.

Mitch got up and took the basin back to the tub, emptying the dirty water and replacing it with fresh supplies. When he returned to our room, he asked me to trade places with him and to put his good foot in the basin. I did. He asked me to massage it. I did. He asked me to put his clubfoot into the basin. I did. He asked me to massage it. I did. And while I massaged his foot he told me the story of Dr. Ignacio Ponseti.

"When he escaped from Franco's Spain during the

Spanish Civil War, he made sure his wounded patients could get across the Pyrenees with him."

"Was he a friend of your father?"

"Nah, you could say he came to me via my mother. She never rested about the surgery done on my foot all those years ago and discovered Ponseti in Iowa. He didn't believe in the surgery, didn't like the results. Limps, gimp shoes, and all that. A firm but gentle kind of manipulation, the Ponseti method uses on and off casts and then braces along with the natural flexibility of infant muscles, joints and ligaments to 'make normal' any child who gets to him in time. But when Mom discovered Ponseti, my surgery had done its damage, and my relatively old infrastructure could no longer be so easily teased into normal positions. Big regret for Mom, but I came to like what set me apart. And then with all Mom's Ponseti pamphlets, I got curious. I looked him up and learned about the Spanish Civil War."

While I listened to Mitch tell me how this seemingly gentle doctor resisted Franco in the best way that he could, bringing his patients with him across the border into safety, Mitch in his own gentle way lifted his clubfoot from the basin, patted it dry, pulled me back onto the bed and then positioned himself so he could use his gimp foot to open me up to our morning pleasure. He emptied himself in the more traditional manner only after he made his way to my center with his smooth and recently rinsed and patted dry perfectly abnormal foot gently rocking me to a heavenly orgasm of earthy delights.

In college I figured out that despite my mismatch with Andrea and Cheryl, our conflicting views over the importance of make-up and other issues, I would never leave them. Of course, *they* couldn't figure out how I bypassed sorority rush week and headed straight to a meeting of a group that would start protesting the war. Even Urbana-Champagne, a formerly sleepy campus, perked up with the times.

I got to know Mitch one afternoon when he asked me to help edit a speech he had drafted for an anti-war rally in Ann Arbor the next week. We traveled to Ann Arbor and went to a party after the rally, where I muttered to him about how most of the guys there would have been in fraternities a couple of years ago and that their types would go straight back to them when all this passed.

"What makes you think it will pass?"

"Just think about the demographics of it, Mitch."

He offered me a cigarette, a habit he gave up after college and I still struggle with. After we both lit up, I continued, sensing how Mitch liked my speed talking whether or not he agreed with my analysis.

"Come on, Mitch. The baby boom in its late adolescence. What do young people do? They rebel. And the older generation has given us this war. It's perfect. But what's the country going to look like when we all head into our fifties, and the generational trend moves more conservative?"

My theory unfortunately proved sound. People like Mitch and me, still active, show up at rallies to the bemusement of the young organizers. Some of them revere us, and only a few seem to revile us. A relief, considering the current demographics. You know, this dazzling hip hop generation of anti-oppression politics and spoken word up against the now plodding baby boom generation of socially responsible investing and long-term care insurance.

So, anyway, that night, after the party, after we had sex, Mitch and I talked about the problems with leadership and ego, which lots of women had started to grasp but few men understood. Mitch Kornblum did, and it drew me to him, just like my mother's unnamed sense of God drew my father, the agnostic, to her. I didn't relate to the growing feminist movement. White and middle-class, which its members reminded me, described *my* demographic, they didn't get race or class. So I stayed away, reading Emma's criticism of the suffragettes and seeing too many parallels when I peeked into consciousness raising groups. Yet, like my father, who protested organized religion but nodded in the direction of my mother's sense of the spirit, I became a reluctant feminist. After all, a critique of the patriarchy, if pitched properly, explains a lot. And Mitch got that, bless him.

Mitch and I loved Emma during college and beyond, and we loved each other during college and beyond. Even during our long years apart, I have tried to deny our love, but I can't. You know, when an eraser dries up, refuses to function, you can turn to liquid paper, delete keys, or amnesia. You can even burn the mess. Incinerate it. Shovel it away. Bulldoze it. Blame it. Crucify it. Shame it. Shame on me. What won't disappear? What I can't erase? My Mitch, and my love for him.

Beastie, why must you torture yourself so? What keeps you from Mitch keeps you from Leah and keeps you from you, pobrecita. You can't spend your life talking to ghosts.

You need real people in your life. Live ones. Ones whose flesh still breaks open when a knife or other steely object pushes into it.

How could he talk like that? He's the one who got me mixed up with dead people. How can he criticize me when I could hang this mess on him?

Be careful, Beastie. That's what we're trying to avoid. The crucifixion complex. The "you're responsible; I'm not" brigade.

Sometimes I, like Emma, went on strike. My lack of response did not bother him. He could always read my mind anyway.

So, anyway, when Mitch and I first met, I wooed him with the story of my grandparents following Emma in their day, dragging me to picnics with Jewish and Italian anarchists in the woods on the outskirts of Chicago. Mitch loved *The Guillotine at Work*, the book criticizing state communism that his Poly Sci TA had recommended, so I impressed him with a photo of its author Maximoff and his wife Olga standing beside Ida and Abe at one of those picnics. I didn't really remember Maximoff because he died before I could get to know him, but I remembered his wife Olga, who as a teenager read his writings and fell in love with them and then with him. My mom loved telling me their love story.

"She took up with him in Paris, like Ida did with Abe in Chicago. In America, the four of them traveled to hot springs wherever they could find them and even took a trip out West. They learned to enjoy themselves after they realized that the revolution, the one their beloved Emma promised, would not happen in their lifetime."

During college when I talked to Abe about my generation's dreams, he gently spoke of theirs.

"Well, we thought the revolution was around the corner, also."

"But, Grandpa, your ideas. They're in the air again. We can do it this time."

"We'll see. We'll see."

Then, when I criticized Israel, he simply said to me, "And you think the country *you're* living in, *I'm* living in, is not a settler nation?"

That's all he said. He left me to figure out the rest.

Sometimes I don't know if Ida and Abe knew what to make of Leah and me. That they loved us no one questioned, but their working class, immigrant, anarchist world looked farther away than a country, or the other side of an ocean, from our middle class South Side Chicago life, the one Mom ached for and managed to mold.

While Ida continued to sell lingerie at The Fair store downtown, Abe worked hanging wallpaper for a contractor named Meyer Supulski.

"Meyer, you're killing me!" he'd shout into the phone when Meyer would assign him to new jobs.

Not a lazy man, Abe thought at sixty he deserved a lighter load.

Abe belonged to the union. So on the Saturdays he covered our kitchen and bathroom walls with Mom's choice of wallpaper—a pink, turquoise, and black geometric design in the kitchen; blue and beige stripes in the main bathroom; a black and white sputnik pattern in the powder room—he closed the drapes and pulled down all the shades. He would not let anyone see him, since working on a Saturday violated union rules. He didn't want to break any rules, union or otherwise, because neither he nor Ida could get their citizenship papers, despite their good English and love for America, never mind its disappointments. They feared deportation, what doomed their beloved Emma to exile. Abe's citizenship finally came through, after Ida died, some time during my college years, but he still didn't like that I talked to friends about his anarchist days, about how Clarence Darrow defended him when he refused to serve in World War I—some rules, big enough to break, I guess. He had joined the Wobblies when he landed in Seattle, a nineteen-year-old greenhorn. Darrow won, saying that Abe and others like him had a right to their ideas, or something noble like that.

But what probably kept my grandmother from becoming an American had ignoble origins. After the divorce, my "bio-grandfather" Jack had gotten her arrested because, even though an anarchist, which also did not endear her to the authorities, she sang in a choral group with communist tendencies, apparently a higher crime. Ida had to spend the weekend in jail, and after she didn't show up on Friday evening, my little mother went to bed repeating the prayers that Tommy Sheehan had taught her. He explained that God, probably angry, would keep her mother from her until she converted. All weekend, she followed his instructions on how to recite "Hail Marys." When Ida showed up Monday afternoon after school to let Rosie know what had happened, Rosie tried to tell Ida about God and Mary and redemption, and what Tommy told her.

"My *shepseleh,* if a god exists, he would not want me locked up."

"Then, why, Ma? Why did it happen?"

"Because Pa is very sad."

"And he wanted to make all of us sad, too?"

"Not exactly, my sweetheart."

When my mother told me that story, I got angry at Jack. In fact, I can mark my stance against him from that afternoon. My mother and I were driving to a warehouse on the West Side of the Loop, where a friend of Andrea's mother could get clothes for wholesale prices. As we rode the freight elevator up to the third floor to meet Mrs. Kahn and row after row of leather jackets of all sizes and dyed pastel colors, I thought of my poor little mother waiting and praying, and never, ever getting. And here I stood, picking out the jacket of my choice, powder blue.

"So lucky you are, my *shayna punim.*"

I began to understand what Ida meant when she said that to me. Such a long haul from one-dress-the-whole-school-year to the leather jacket of rich pickings.

And the creaky wooden floor of the wholesale warehouse sat almost another entire ocean apart from the new motel on Stony Island with its swimming pool and chaise lounges. Cheryl's parents had the bright idea of renting a room at the all-modern Rainbow Motel for a whole Saturday. That meant we could use the room to change in and spend the day playing in the pool, jumping off the high dive board, and flirting with boys. Innocent pleasures that the Rainbow must chuckle about from its long ago past now that its rooms have gone to seed and hourly rates.

Chicago summers. Maybe my love for them comes from my poor circulation keeping me ten degrees colder

53

than everyone else, a natural air conditioning system. Of course, it makes the winters worse. Leah says I should move to California, that Randi and Michael would follow. I tell her I cannot leave this place and the rewards winter offers if you stick them out. You can't enjoy a perfect spring day in the same way if you haven't suffered through a miserable winter. Then, after spring, comes wide, open summer with no jackets or sweaters, no scarves, no burdens, or so you can pretend. The leaves bleeding their glory in the fall. Nothing like it, nothing at all. And the stories you can collect. Weather builds character.

"We have weather in Los Angeles," Leah liked to remind met

"Yeah. Warm and warmer."

"But you love the heat."

"I love suffering more. It helps assuage the guilt and makes me feel like I've earned a beautiful day."

Beastie, I don't know what to do with you. Poor Leah and everyone else are sick of your song of the four seasons along with your politics. Give up your rhapsody in frozen blue and grand finale of gorgeous green. Give up your search for who knows what perfect world that does not exist. Remember what Abe said. Instead of the messiah, or his non-religious equivalent, came the war and the Republicans. JFK, a minor blip, and a manufactured one at that.

So we're not doing so well right now, but you sent me Emma, who never gave up, as sad as it got, as hellish as it seemed. Hanging on has its merits, Danny. Remember the old lady who used to run the newsstand by the library, on Randolph Street, next to the stairs going down to the train? Bundled up for all kinds of weather, layers of jackets and more than one scarf, wool cap, and old galoshes. Not many teeth left but lots of hair. Mom used to treat me with a comic book from her stand for the ride on the IC. The plucky Illinois Central made famous by a song or two. Just another way to get us back to the South Side in those days.

What is your point, Beastie?

Well, in those days, people didn't give up. That lady on the corner never gave up. She stood there every day, even the kind of days my dad's father joked about having to chip the milkman off the corner.

Oh, Beastie. You sound so old.

Maybe I am.

And soooo self-righteous.

I would not dispute Danny's assessment, but that woman standing there represented what I loved about Chicago. People stood for something. You might not like the stands they took, but you knew that they'd tell you how they felt, what they thought. And they weren't afraid of a good argument or two, or more.

For years people have gone to California to make a fortune, whether in gold, real estate, Hollywood, or some other scheme, but they also come to lose their past, the intensity of old relations. They say good-bye to friends and family who knew them from birth, people they can't bullshit, who love them no matter what, except that along with that love come regular visits and phone calls, promises kept, commitments honored, and, yes, verbal knives stuck in and turned once in a while. So life is easier in the land where the verb "to pencil in" took root, to the extent that anything takes root there. And then there's the selection process. Those who can't take these fly-by-night-gone-by-day relationships head back East. It's evolutionary. The survival of the flakiest.

Long ago, however, Leah predicted it would spread across the country like other trends brought to us courtesy of the have-a-nice-day golden state. And I have to admit she got that right. Although people answer messages at a much higher rate in Chicago, and friends and lovers, married or not, leave each other at far lower rates compared to San Diego, Los Angeles, Santa Barbara and San Francisco, even in Chicago we're moving forward into the art of the penciled in calendar. That way there's no mess if something better turns up.

But not me. Instead of getting the hang of it, I hang on, longer than anyone feels comfortable with. That's why no one understood how I could leave Mitch. I knew why. Deep in the rocky bottom creek of our love, I knew.

Mom liked Mitch right away when I brought him home at the beginning of the summer just before her un-remission became official. Why not say "the cancer returned"? Because when you live long enough to picture parole and the gate shuts down on your dreams, you keep fantasizing about your first meal outside for a while longer. Death in its grim certitude and sinking melancholy gets a brush off; even I can get the hang of that.

Mom and Mitch, you could say, drew up a pact that summer; their only mistake, not inviting me to the negotiations. Mom, with the talent of the dead, now knows where they went wrong.

I could arrange for your mother to visit your ex-husband.
All right, Danny, now *you* stop.

I loved my mother the way some daughters do, safe and secure, and desperate. The idea of losing her frightened me, even as a little girl, when the world she created made loss seem impossible. I remember going with her to Marshall Field's one day after morning kindergarten let out. In the middle of the week, we caught the Jeffrey local on 100th Street, got off at 71st, and made our way to the Loop via the IC. Later, came the Jeffrey Express, which kept the poor, black neighborhoods out of sight for the South Side whites. Now they call it the Jackson Park Express to make it sound more high class. And the whole South Side is black now except for Hyde Park, where we liberals—some white and some black—mix.

Beastie, stop!

Well, it's true.

Just get on with the story.

All right, all right. So that afternoon we shared one of her famous chicken salad sandwiches sitting on a stone bench in the little garden on the north side of the Art Institute and then crossed Michigan Avenue to make our way to Field's. Shopping for a new chair for our little living room in the four-room house my parents had bought a few years after the war ended, we took the elevator to "Furniture" on the third floor and moved from one to another chair with an eager salesman's assistance.

I loved how people looked at my mother, the way this salesman did. It wasn't just her classic Jewish beauty looks (after Bess Myerson became the still one and only Jewish Miss America, the *very* year the war ended, our girls got looked at in a new way), but her elegance and her way of making everyone around her feel elegant, too. Classy, charming, disarming. That was Mom.

So after my mother and the salesman finished examining a particular chair, discussing its merits and possible limits for our little house, and moved on to the next, I would sink myself into the one they had just turned from, sure that Mom should choose this one, each one appearing more luxurious than the last. Finally, the salesman wrote some numbers on the back of his business card, and Mom took it and thanked him while she slid it into a side pocket of her purse, promising she'd ask for him the following week when she'd make her final decision. She didn't tell the salesman she needed to discuss it with her husband. Looking back now, I know she didn't want to disappoint that salesman now clearly smitten with her. Sure, he was the one who was supposed to close the sale, but in Mom's world, no one had a chance. She opened and closed every event, and her fans, both family and strangers, would not have missed any one of them.

Next, that day, in long ago 1952 Rosie history, we rode the elevator up to the sixth floor where a large lounge offered shoppers a respite and a place to smoke a cigarette. The chairs and couches there, made of thick brown leather, seemed so different from the green and gold and beige jobs on "Three." Mom liked earth colors, and so did I. I liked whatever she liked, I went wherever she went, I spoke–or tried to, at least–however she spoke. I was enchanted. In love with my mother. No one can make that go away, even me when I try. It got better when I realized that my mother truly *was* beautiful and smart. Other kids thought so, too. She knew more than the other mothers. And she was always such a good date. Funny and pointing out every little detail of the day to pay attention to and hold on to, for later. So, when she died, desperation set in for good.

I would visit the Art Institute, in the days of "Free" every day, all day, just to stand in front of the Lorado Taft sculpture called "The Solitude of the Soul." For years it kept bright and humming by itself beside the grand stairway in the central hall, where it stood the day Ida bent down to whisper to her Rosie.

"See, sweetheart, how strong Taft's hands were, to make such a thing. This is the best one here, Rosie. Just look."

And what did she love? Two men and two women, each with distance between them—one couple holding hands, one man sobbing on the shoulder of the woman holding hands with the other man, and the second woman almost ignored, though touching both men, like the other woman, the one you're supposed to notice. A working class, immigrant mother passing on her love for art and her love for life and for sex, her experience of how love never completely satisfies, how something always remains missing, perhaps just a small thing, but some thing.

No matter how much we love, it leaves us bereft. Maybe not in tribal cultures, I don't know, but in my culture, the one I grew up in and my grandmother passed on to me through my own mother, a little something goes missing. People sculpt and paint and sing and sometimes go crazy to ease the pain of a broken heart, to bridge that lonely place between souls, the fact that each body does remain its own house. "Come on-a my house. My house a come on." Rosemary Clooney's remarkable invitation. Who could pass that up? Or Eartha Kitt's cover? Now *that* woman knew how to enter a house.* Make love, not war, and all that.

Thankfully, some mention of popular culture, Beatrice, and real sex, not just the marble kind. And you can't pass up the opportunity for a political plug. Well, all right.

So, anyway, when they moved "Soul" from its original place, long after they had moved other favorite pieces from their locations I knew as a child, I mourned its loss for a while, even as I followed it to its new hall, a room devoted to other neoclassical white marble sculptures. I had to adjust. It was now one among many. But such a one. And that's the kind of mother I had. Such a one.

My Rosie, Rosie Kleinbaum Rubenstein, turned our rooms on Paxton Avenue into a small palace of loving arts. She made sure that every meal had a vegetable and some protein. She bought baskets of cherries in the summer and sweet apples when school started in the fall. The palace of Rosie and Howard. Dad seeded the front and back yards. The black dirt dotted with green sprouts responded to his faithful watering. Every day Dad would unroll the green garden hose and water the lawn, first the front, and then the back, after he got home from teaching and before he'd leave for law school at night. Mom had gotten pregnant again, and although she promised she would take no extreme measures like she had with me, on bed rest for six months, it looked like this baby would hold tight until its time to pop. Dad didn't want to have to support a family of four on a high school teacher's salary, and he didn't want Mom to go back to work. He figured that a law practice would loosen up the family budget.

---

* Eartha Kitt spoke against the Vietnam War at a White House luncheon.

That spring Mom and I planted flowers around the stone patio Dad had set behind our back door. When the flowers came up, they reached above my knees and formed a little forest that protected our stone island, where Mom sat reading while I played with friends, sometimes trading cards. I remember coveting one card in particular: a lush black cocker spaniel on a bright red background that Gary Kagan refused to give up. I promised I'd give him a kiss if he'd trade it to me. I waited until Rosie had gone inside to make some lemonade, somehow sensing that she would not have approved of my selling myself for a card. I won my prize. Who knows where I learned that kind of trade? Did Gary come up with the idea and I merely complied? Much later, when some guy thought he had used me one night and I carefully explained the mutuality of our pleasure and use, I remembered the kiss for the card as *my* idea. A little five-year-old girl pleased with her acquisition and proud of her power. Such innocence I carried with me for years, until I crashed into stories of girls getting poked at by their brothers and fathers and grandfathers and uncles and mothers' boyfriends under the covers, under the cover of night. For them the sexual liberation movement had a different loop to it. For them the world, though it could heal, never would seem quite right.

My world in the trading card days seemed perfect, especially after Leah arrived. The morning of her birth, a fresh summer day two weeks before my own birthday, I rode up and down the street on my new two-wheeler shouting to all the kids on the sidewalk and the ones still lingering on their front porches that I had a new baby sister. Finally, I had joined the legions of children through-out the ages, and especially in the fifties, who had sib-lings. No longer an only child, I could say "my sister this" and "my sister that." A new kind of heaven for me.

Okay, one time they caught me pushing in her soft, sweet, unformed little baby nose and disapproved, but I could tell Leah liked it by how she giggled. A more true and deliberate yet mostly unconscious act of aggression came a year later when I showed Leah how to do a som-ersault which got me time in my room to "consider" my actions. Somehow the demonstration must have gone off course. Leah simply thrilled me. She still does. But I would be lying if I didn't say she also frightens me.

Sibling rivalries, or other minor challenges, could not compare to the silent shadow hovering over us, which my parents hid from me, and which Leah, still a baby, would know nothing of except through history books, and only left leaning ones, the ones I would drag her to when I dis-covered them in college.

Then, all those years ago, when the hunt was on or as it finally finished, I remember the morning Howard opened the newspaper and hurrahed as he read Rosie the story about Joe McCarthy's demise. They kept the Rosenbergs from me, but this one seeped out. Shocked that my peace loving parents cheered at someone's death, I had more to learn about them.

One afternoon, a couple of years before Leah arrived, I climbed onto the bus in front of Mom and sat down and stared at the face of the only black woman on the bus, the only black person I remember seeing until then. Mom explained I should not stare, which I knew, but this person looked so different. And I could feel something wrong from my mother, the tight, clammy shame of segregated Chicago of the fifties. The woman on the bus, someone's "cleaning lady," not even a true neighbor.

Later my parents would explain the unfairness of racism and the importance of fighting for social justice. And, then, a few years after Leah's birth, Rosie and Howard hired a cleaning lady for *our* home, Violet. She became a confidante to my mother when she got sick, but she's gone from our lives now. A quiet, shy black woman who came to our house once a week for fifteen years to help Mom with the "heavy" work and Dad with all the work after Mom died. "A petty bourgeois family," that's how Abe described us, even though he loved us and kept most of his criticisms to himself.

And the liberal families keep their servants to themselves. Notice your family did not call Violet your maid, somehow making it all seem less high class. But listen, Beatrice, although your parents exploited Violet, they treated her well, with a certain respect, which she most likely appreciated. I'm not excusing the exploitation. They could not have afforded Violet's services if they paid her what she deserved. We both know that. Yet they tumbled into their times, without noticing where or how far they had fallen. It happens. You don't think all these years dead haven't softened me? I don't condone, but I don't condemn.

Maybe, Emma, but I wonder how much Violet appreciated my parent's "respect." "Violet" to them; "Mr. and Mrs. Rubenstein" to her. No social security or health insurance, the required bags of old clothes. It makes me sick.

And what makes me sicker, this constant hairshirt. Danny's right. You need some peace. You need some solace. But that, young lady, you will have to provide for yourself.

I'm not so young.

I was trying to be polite.

My parents did their best, pushed themselves as far as they could go, set up a good foundation, and, yet, none of us gets away clean or free. Even when we steam off the sludge, our wicked, wicked souls languish in the slow moving rivers of complication and fear. So my father picked up what he could from the dust, swept away the guilty parties, eventually graduated from law school and began a new career at nearly fifty. He rented a small office in the Monadnock Building at 53 W. Jackson and began what later turned into Rubenstein and Rubenstein. He kept business for small businesses and families, helped people out with adoptions, managed estates, drafted wills, took on some personal injury cases.

All out of the dark brick building that made Chicago famous for standing the tallest in the world, around the same time the city disgraced itself by bullying the anarchists at Haymarket Square. I work out of the Monadnock today. They've refurbished it, polished it up to its former glory, added in fresh new glory, and then made it a landmark. This narrow slab of granite and terra cotta, preening itself, now part of architectural tours and city history.

As I take the elevator up to the eighth floor, I think of my dad and all those days he flew up there during the era of Rosie and Howard and all those years he slowly and sadly followed the floor numbers moving from 1 to 2, and so on, until the car shuttled to 8, and he sighed while the door pulled open, and he began another day with no Rosie at the end of the line when he called home. Dad brightened when I finished law school and joined his practice, dragging our first immigration case to the files of R and R, our family partnership stationed between Jackson Street and the sky. Dad stuck around on a part-time basis, guiding me while I pulled together something that looked like a socially conscious law firm, working with hungry and tired Mexican and Central American immigrants and then learning how to keep one hand in the money-making world of visas for tech workers that America yearned for, pretending to be free.

Beastie, I appreciate all the work you have done on behalf of my people, but you cannot overlook the mitzvahs *your father performed for the little people, maybe not fresh from the border or the boat but not exactly blue bloods either. Howard deserves some credit for the way he sat there after the funeral and told the widow to come downtown, he would help her out, or for how he put the right clause into the contract to protect the young woman going into business and negotiating a lease from a lizard, and for having the good sense to follow an ambulance or two, so you and Leah could have all the winter coats you would ever need.*

You're right, Danny. My father, a *mensch*, I will never deny it. He loved, and he lived, and he grieved, and he got some *naches*, and then he died. And I did not remark of him enough while he walked among us, so I will not neglect him now. Friend of Ernie, lover of Rosie, father to Beatrice and Leah. Grandfather to Randi and Michael and Raoul. Savior of little people who needed a lawyer in a jam. Howard Rubenstein, my dad. Son of Simon Lazarus and grandson of Hyam Mordecai.

Hyam, you should know, carried Jews across the border to safety, arranged for papers and bribes. When I wrote his story, and the editors of the *Brennan Express* wanted to publish it, I got called down to the Vice-Principal's office. A Jew, Mr. Bass, sat across the desk from me and so easily, too easily, called up the nerve to tell me they could not publish the story unless I removed the fact that my grandfather was a Jew smuggling Jews.

"We all get along here, Beatrice. Jews, Mexicans, Negroes, Poles, Serbs, Lutherans, Catholics; we're a melting pot, known for it. So we can't single out one group for heroism. Just leave off that your grandfather was Jewish, just leave out specific references to Jews. Call him Eastern European, and we'll publish it."

"But, Mr. Bass, if I take out that part, there's no point to the story. The Jews fled the pogroms. Many of them needed help crossing the border. I can't leave it out."

"Then no story, Beatrice."

"You're right, Mr. Bass. No story."

That winter I helped to found the Human Relations Club at our school. In the spring we took the bus downtown to a conference on Michigan Avenue at the Commonwealth Edison offices where I remember Chuck Stone, the editor of *The Defender*, Chicago's black newspaper, carefully impressing on the audience of student leaders concerned about race relations how every Negro had at least latent hatred for white people. Shocked, disturbed, hurt, I didn't understand. I didn't hate *them*. Why would they hate *me*? Later I would understand how Stone helped me steal past a border that day, one that Mr. Bass guarded with his frightened life.

Mom thought Dad should go in and give Mr. Bass "what for." Dad told her I'd taken care of it myself. I'll never forget that moment when he looked at Mom and then at me and said "Rosie, Bicie handled it fine. She fought her own battle and won."

Somehow getting censored didn't feel like winning to me, but landing my dad's approval like that, well, it's a moment to live for. Howard Rubenstein declares you the winner? You go down in history.

I loved the stories about my dad and his brother and sister growing up on the West Side of Chicago. His younger brother took offense when gentiles called him dirty names, but he wore glasses and didn't have my dad's athletic skills.

"So your father," as my Aunt Gertrude told the story, "would be sitting at home reading a book when Reuben would come in furious, telling Howard he had to go out there and show them they couldn't call Jews names. Your dad, always patient, put down his book, got himself out the door past our incensed brother, and carefully, and as quietly as possible, beat the kid up. Then he'd come back in the house, pick up his book, and finish off the afternoon in peace."

My dad's family struggled, but tragedy didn't heave them a permanent blow the way it did my mom's.

You see, Rosie knew from an early age what it felt like to start out the morning normal, like everyone else, living your regular life, and then in one shrieking second, it all collapses. You survive, sometimes the cruelest injury of all. Marked, you never cross back to normal. You look the same, strangers don't know you're lost, but you live exiled, far away from everyone for a long time. In the middle of the month of April in the year 1919, my mother had just turned six years old when she learned the lesson of waking up happy and going to bed terrified.

That fall the White Sox threw the World Series. People blamed a Jew, Arnold Rothstein, for fixing it. And he probably did. Not a good mark on us, an embarrassment similar to the present neo-cons who claim to speak for all of us. Unlike Mr. Bass back at Brennan who refused to say our name, they play our suffering like the card that doesn't quit.

1919. A bad year for Rosie's little family, and a bad year for Chicago. That summer, a race riot broke out when a black teen-ager drowned after crossing an unofficial line at 29th Street that kept the beaches separated. At thirteen, I learned the term *de facto* and how to distinguish it from the *de jure* variety of segregation. A matter of practice or law, either way, crossing lines can get you killed.

1947. The year I came clawing through the air, landing, relieved and panting, in some doctor's arms, Jackie Robinson broke through one of those lines and survived. A Negro playing for the Dodgers. Who calls 1919 the bad year and 1947 the good? In whose family's history? Endless scores, infinite scores, secret scores, scoreboards blown to bits in the sky. A good or bad year? Good people? Bad people? A good solution? The final solution. Extremes, proportions of right, wrong, and relative merit of that peace plan, or this. Leah's perspective or mine. Depends on whose history you believe. Which version? 1948.1967.1982. Or just the facts. How many dead bodies on this border or that? No one would defend a holocaust or a genocide, but they'll say you don't have the whole truth, *their* side of the story. Listen to the Turks talk about the Armenians or the people who bet that the Sox would win in 1919 give you a piece of theirs about the Jews.

Basta, mi abuelita, *with your aches and your pains. Your complaints and your continuous chatter. I'm feeling you, Bi-cie, about Ernie and the rest of them, but you need to calm down. Let Emma give you a massage. Let her put you to bed. Please take a rest before I myself collapse from your talk without end.*

And so it goes with Danny and Emma, my protectors and defenders. But this problem of sides has not seen its resolution yet. Splitters. The people who name this one *good* and that one *bad*. This child, *my favorite,* and that one, *trouble.*

Beast-ie!

And before I can add one more sad story to the ones I have just told, I'm floating in a small soft hole filled with warm water in the mountains of Mexico and awaken the next morning with liquid limbs and an uncluttered mind. The Zen of Emma and a good night's sleep.

Journals: 2

And, so, at each Passover, though I'd hoped to come closer to Leah, I saw her moving away from me, preoccupied and less engaged. She still roamed the flea markets, and when Raoul started college, she spent endless hours reading. Eli called a few times a year to tell me that he worried about her, but when I suggested therapy, he cringed.

"That's not the answer, Bicie. It goes deeper than that."

"But, Eli, that's what therapy is supposed to do, go deeper."

"I can't explain. Just make sure the two of you are good at Passover. Take walks. She likes that. Bring her to the lake. She likes the park. Take her to the Art Institute."

And for the years we went to Santa Monica.

"She likes the ocean. Take your shoes off. Walk along the sand with her barefoot. Don't discuss politics. Tell her you love her."

I began to realize that Eli, in trying to prevent one tragedy, might have been creating another. Through his carefully composed codes, I got the message that he feared for Leah's life. But in keeping her from disappearing, finally, he was keeping her from herself and from us. I was only partially right. Eli knew about the journals. I didn't, until a year ago when he made his usual pre-Passover phone call.

"Bicie, I need to tell you about something."

"Leah?"

"It's nothing new, but I've never told you about the writing. You need to know."

"Eli, that's great. I mean, that she's writing again."

"Bicie, I'm not so sure. For the past ten years, she pours into these journals. The content, Bicie, has begun to frighten me."

"So you've read them."

"I've read them, Bicie. I had to. I had to know. I needed some explanation for her behavior. Her withdrawal. With Raoul she would be the old Leah, and sometimes, probably enough times at first so that I didn't even catch on, she would be the person I fell in love with, but then, a stranger, a polite, careful stranger, Bicie. And now the stranger wanders through our house bumping into the old Leah once in a while. At the flea markets she picks up. But that's it. At Passover, with Raoul there and the rest of you, she returns. So you wouldn't have known. She returns and puts up her usual defense of Israel and cooks a meal to die for. But that's what I'm afraid of. I think part of her is preparing to die, Bicie. I've read the journals."

"So what is she writing about?"

"Holocausts."

"Holocausts?"

"Yes."

And then he talked about their life together, and Leah's life apart. She and Eli still had sex. I don't know why Eli needed to tell me that, except I think he tried to show whatever part of normalcy she had retained. She talked to him about his classes, still interested in the stories of his students. But she started dropping her friends. She just didn't call them back. To Rhoda, who persisted, she became rude, actually shouting at her to leave her alone one night when she called. Rhoda kept in touch with Eli, checking in every so often.

"I know of a good therapist, Eli."

"Out of the question, Rhoda."

"How about anti-depressants? People have been having success with them."

"Never!"

"I've been to an herbalist. If we can get Leah over there, she thinks she can help. She's very intuitive, Eli. Gentle. There's an acupuncturist and a homeopathic doctor in her office. She'll figure out what would work best."

"Rhoda. You are becoming desperate."

"Well, aren't you?"

"Yes."

"Then you have to break in."

So Eli did. He believed that with the amount of writing he saw Leah doing, she would have at least a box full, maybe more, of journals. He couldn't find them anywhere in the house. The old satchel she used to travel with had disappeared, so he figured that she must have been keeping the journals in the storage space she rented out for furniture she picked up at flea markets and then slowly restored, putting some in their house and selling some back. The family always used the same code for locks and passwords, the number of the apartment Leah and Eli lived in during graduate school: 1329. He tried it, and it worked.

That first box of journals contained Leah's reflections on every piece of holocaust literature she could find at the

UCLA library. She brought none of the books home, but she carefully documented each one with call number and publishing citation.

"Who knows where she read them at? Maybe in that storage room, Bicie, all alone. She kept a rocking chair there. She called one journal 'Surviving' and another 'Surrendering'. She examined how cruelty and brutality, compressed in a few short years, thrust themselves against millions. She wrote how she refused to submit to Hannah Arendt's charge of the 'banality of evil', saying that it told only part of the story. She struggled with issues of moral choice, collective responsibility, accountability, hatred, evil, 'monsterdom.'" She kept moving back and forth.

"If I weren't so struck by the isolation, the secret hoarding, the emotional torture she was causing herself, I would have been enthralled. Sometimes I forgot my worries and floated through her writing–like gold, like the silver she collects. I'd forgotten how much I loved her poetry and her ability to tear through an Emily Dickinson poem and come up breathing. You see, Bicie, some of the journals represented pure literary criticism by Leah Rubenstein, the lapsed academic. She discussed the poetry of Nelly Sachs and Paul Celan. She devoted an entire journal to letters she wrote to Anne Frank describing how her writing had saved a generation from 'restless unknowing'. That's how she described it. She wrote to Frank as if she were a young student, the kind the professor knows she must nurture because a voice like that should not go silent. As if somehow Anne Frank had presented herself to Leah asking, 'Is this good? Can I do this? Will people like it?'"

My sister created a life for herself inside those journals. No wonder she didn't need any friends, or me. And so I learned about the first box of journals, and then the second.

"Bicie, she made a comparison study of Viktor Frankl and Primo Levi. That one had an outline on the inside front and back covers with cross-outs and arrows, and then she plunged into her composition, clear and focused, worthy of publication. She didn't believe Levi committed suicide. In another journal she wrote a play in which the two voices, Frankl and Levi mirrored the views of the two survivors, arguing about which qualities a person needed to outlive torture, starvation, humiliation."

"Eli..."

"Five years, ago, Bicie, the journals took a turn."

"So you continued to read? And you didn't tell her?"

"I told myself I was monitoring Leah's health. I kept it private, just between Leah and me, except that, yes, Bicie, Leah didn't know. But, Bicie, she used our number for the lock. I think at some point she knew I had let myself into her secrets. I told Rhoda nothing of the contents except that I thought Leah had found a way to take care of herself, that Rhoda didn't need to worry. We talk regularly. She is a real friend."

"And, so, Eli, the turn the journals took?"

"She started writing about the other people who had died in the camps, especially the gypsies. She was very interested in the gypsies, the Roma people."

"Yes, yes."

"She started out slowly just recording what she had learned, but then she twisted into this awful hole of guilt. 'Why don't Jewish historians talk more about all the others?' That sort of thing."

At first, I thought I could listen to Eli's oddly calm voice for hours, but I suddenly felt tired, like I had been walking for a long time and needed to sit down, like I could not take one more step. I felt heavy, and afraid. I also started to worry that Eli himself had entered into Leah's world, but I wanted to be more focused when I addressed this.

"Eli, can we continue this tomorrow night?"

"Of course, Bicie, I wasn't thinking. I've had years to sit with this."

This is good, Beatrice. You need to take care of yourself. Stop now. Call him back when you're ready. You have a lot to understand here. These curious details and broad running evidence of your sister's unraveling will cause a gasp. But you must understand you have not lost her. Slowly let the breath out. You will find you feel much more full than usual.

Emma's words comforted because I was afraid that I would never find a way back to Leah, that she had submerged herself, the classic story of the researcher living too long with mind destroying subject matter. I slept hard that night and woke up the next morning with a feeling of eager anticipation, not the dread I went to bed with.

I called my friends without telling them anything. I just needed to hear their voices. It would ground me. I got Andrea's home answering machine and Cheryl's voice mail at work.

Mitch knew, when I reached him, that evolving or not, some emergency had surfaced. He didn't pry, but he wouldn't let me go.

"You sound pretty wound up. Since for once we can do real time, may I ask you to a real dinner tonight?"

"Couldn't make it until after eight."

"Listen, just come over when you're done with work. I'll keep some soup simmering."

"All right, my long lost love and parenting partner."

When I called Mitch that, I always thought of Paul, not lost but gone. He's the one I could talk to about all of this. Leah intrigued him. Even though he'd skip Passover, he always made sure to come over when Leah and Eli visited. He didn't mind Leah's Zionism. Paul, my lover. My former law professor. My eventual law partner. And then my ex-lover, ex-partner, and forever friend. Two Americans. A Jew from the South Side and a Palestinian from Bridgeview.

"You don't think I have a few relatives who would like to run the Zionists into the sea? We all have our extremists, and your Leah, like my family members, are good, decent people."

Paul liked talking to Leah about poetry. He gave her a book of Mahmoud Darwish's poems. She returned the next year we were all in Chicago with Emily Dickinson for him.

"I give you a living man. Why do you stretch so far back?"

"You gave me your strength, Paul. I give you mine. I thought of bringing Nelly Sachs, but I think my sister would object to her Zionist leanings. She's one of my sustainers, shares a birthday with Dickinson."

"Twins."

"You could say."

"I know Sachs. Nobel winner. She died before things got so bad. Who knows where she'd be now, Leah?"

"Paul…"

I stopped my sister before she could get into an argument with him, though that was unlikely. Paul was simply teasing her. Gently seeing if she would open. But nothing was gentle about my sister's beliefs about Israel. Nothing flexible. Nothing uncertain. At least nothing that I knew of.

So, now, Beatrice, you may take some more deep breaths and then call the person you do need to talk with, not your friends, not your ex-husband here or your ex-lover in Palestine. Call your brother-in-law, the breaker of code and confidence.

Emma had a lot of integrity, which I identified with, trying to keep myself as moral and ethical as possible in the updated world of new values, new strategies, the art of penciling in and scratching out.

There is no excuse for betrayal. On this I will not budge.

But, Emma, when someone you love has made it to the edge…

She didn't respond. Nothing. Silence. I felt cut off. Danny, too, refused to speak. I didn't get it. On my own, this time, both training wheels raised off the ground, out of sight and sound. So I called Eli, a living person who would answer me and who deserved my attention more than anyone else, except for Leah herself.

"Okay, Eli. I'm ready for the rest."

"There is no rest, or no rest for Leah, at least."

"After the gypsies…"

"Yes, Eli."

"She started skipping around. She moved forward to Bosnia. That was hard for her. You know Leah, never a hateful person. She had as much feeling for the Muslims as she had for any of the rest. When she read about the rape camps and then wrote about them...well, this was hard for me to read."

"I understand, Eli."

What world had my sister entered? What punishment did she need to endure? And why? What could I say to Eli? What would I say to Leah when she arrived? Now that I knew, how could I keep quiet?

"Bicie, it goes on. She has torn her heart open about Africa. Rwanda. Darfur. She bleeds and bleeds. The poetry..."

"Poetry? Oh right, you said she began writing poems again."

"Yes, starting with the Roma she moved into poetry. A few lines here and there, at first, and then she began to piece them together. I'm no judge, but I believe it's significant, Bicie. Sometimes I needed a break. I couldn't go to the closet. That's what I called the storage space, the closet. After a month or so, I'd be back. I worried too much to stay away. There is a journal, Bicie–I call it the index–an entire journal that simply lists one atrocity after another, each with a line to itself and then next to it whether or not she had completed that tragedy's volume. I could unwind them for you: the dirty wars, Chile, Argentina; the killing fields, Cambodia; the massacres, Plaza Tlatelolco, Tiananmen Square; the rape camps, Bosnia; mass rapes, Congo; sex trafficking/human trafficking, Eastern Europe, Asia, Latin America; forced relocations, suicides, political assassinations, torture and murder of journalists; the disappeared everywhere. She didn't use the computer, Bicie, except to make contributions to Amnesty International, Human Rights Watch, Survival International, Reporters without Borders. I became a spy, Bicie, and when I saw that she had started to read about the Israeli torture of Palestinians, I knew I would need to become more. In that journal I heard a new voice, blank almost, detached, as if she herself had been tortured, split, separated from the Leah I know and love..."

So last Passover, in Santa Monica, I watched Leah. I watched how she moved and how she spoke and what she said and what she didn't say. By then I knew enough not to talk about the latest atrocity performed by the Israeli government or soldiers or both. And, frankly, instead of all the innocent children lost, I could think only of losing one single child, my baby sister.

We got through the Seder. We took our usual walk along the beach. Somehow when Leah and I walk along the beach with the wide-open Pacific at our side, we dissolve back into our early years, when nothing came between us. I knew I should just let the peacefulness settle us, even while the journals pestered me. Though Leah would not, of course, talk about them, she did create a crack for me to enter into.

"Bicie, sometimes I think a lot about the war."

"Vietnam? Iraq?" I didn't mean to be facetious, but I wanted Leah to lead.

"No Bicie. The *War*. The one that killed all of our relatives."

"The ones who didn't made it to America."

"Yes, Bicie, those ones. I think about Dad's friend, Ernie, how those guys tried to stop Franco. They didn't stand a chance, but that they *took* a stand means a lot in the history of our kind."

"Our kind?"

"Humans. Beings. The two legged *mensches* who picked themselves up one day and decided they could do something about something."

"Got it."

"You know, Rhoda's mother participated in incidents of sabotage in the Belgian factory where she worked."

"I didn't know that."

"Rhoda's proud of her."

"I would be too. Leah, before Dad died, he used to talk about all the forms the Resistance took. Thank God he never lost short-term memory, but he liked dwelling in his long-term more and more. The history teacher returned. He'd lecture about the non-violent resisters like Rhoda's mom, and then all those farmers hiding Jews, and downed American pilots, the *violent* resisters. You know, there was a girl in our neighborhood whose dad apparently had been killed in the Warsaw Ghetto Uprising. She was pretty quiet. Do you remember her? Her name was Iris or Lily, I can't remember right now, speaking of memory."

"I know exactly who you're talking about. Iris Feldstein. Mom hired her to babysit me when you went to college. Iris and I decided I was definitely too old for a babysitter, but she could use the money. She's the one who gave me my first book of Dickinson poems, one of those abridged versions published in the fifties. She kept living at home with her mother even after she graduated from the University of Chicago. She became a translator. I think she was about six or seven years older than you."

"That'd be about right."

"I don't know what ever happened to her, but the sadness that she and her mother carried with them everywhere they went affected me. I felt so guilty. Our happy family. Her broken one. Then when Mom got sick the last time, Iris was the kindest of all the people in the neighborhood. She understood. When I pleaded with her how it was hopeless, what was the point, she turned to me, stared directly into my eyes, and said 'Leah, remember this, it is always important to go down fighting.'"

"Yeah, that's what her dad did."

"He got her and her mom smuggled out first."

"You think some of their sadness was all that survivor guilt?"

"You *think*?"

I knew it would not be fair for me to tell Leah that I actually remembered Iris very well, that, in fact, I had run across her name in a group of women protesting the occupation of the West Bank and Gaza. I could not use this now. It would not be fair.

"You know, some of the Jewish resistance fighters, the ones in the Ghetto were members of the Irgun."

"I know, Leah"

"They fought back."

"They did."

I had to let this go. In earlier years I would have used my card about where the daughter of one of those resisters ended up on the question of the Israeli Occupation. I would have talked about the atrocities the Irgun and Stern Gang perpetrated on Palestinians. I would bring up the Deir Yassin massacre, how the...

And you won't, right Beastie?

Right, Danny.

Leah would never, ever have condoned that.

Yes, but what she has condoned can lead to that and worse, and has.

And this is not what her struggle with the journals is about?

You're right. I will shut up.

For which I am grateful.

When we got back to the house, Leah realized that she needed to pick up something for dinner. I wanted to help get the house ready, but Eli interrupted my plans. He seemed eager to deliver some good news, something Leah hadn't mentioned during our walk.

"Bicie, stop with all of your silver polishing and furniture dusting. It's just enough you are here. And, guess what, Bicie? Something you'll never believe. An old graduate school friend, a professor now at USC, called last month. I gave Leah the message, thinking she'd never call her back, but she did. Joanie asked her to teach a seminar on Dickinson this fall when she goes on sabbatical, and, Bicie, she accepted. Leah accepted."

"Maybe something has shifted, Eli."

"We can only hope."

So we finished Passover in Santa Monica, and I kept my big mouth shut. I didn't talk to Eli again until last month. Before that, we exchanged e-mails as he kept me up with Leah's state.

"In and out, Bicie. Open one day, closed the next. Each week, the day before the seminar, she seems to open. Like a flower, Bicie, and then the day after, she closes down again. But you were right. Something has shifted."

I wondered if anything could shift between us about Palestine. Her resolute Zionism. My persistent anti-Zionism. If only she could see. I wanted her to read the e-mails that my friend Deborah sends every time she goes to Palestine to defend house demolitions. The land seizures. The checkpoints. The roadblocks. And now this wall that steals more land and divides Palestinian from Palestinian. Leah doesn't seem to pay attention that I never gave support to the suicide bombers that began after the sham of Oslo became apparent and then intensified, provoked, some still say, by Sharon stomping around the Temple Mount.

Bombs instead of rocks. A strategic and a humanitarian mistake. Yes, Israelis kill civilians. Yes, they commit state terrorism, but Jews at one time, when they had no guns, really could play the role of righteous victim. Now they've lost it and have turned their victimhood into a profession, dicing it up for power and profit whenever they get the chance. But the Palestinians have gained no real benefit from the suicide attacks, and they're losing the moral advantage along with a generation of martyrs.

Leah knows I know all of this, but she acts somehow like I support them, these bombers. I know better. It saddens me that she thinks I don't. I wish she could read Deborah's messages and meet people like Blume, the friend of my mother's friend Evelyn.

So, Blume. We need some story here, my dear. Enough with the philosophizing and moralizing. You will put them to sleep.

I met Blume last summer when Evelyn, Mom's only surviving friend, invited me to a Millennium Park concert. At 86, Evelyn still maintains a large though quickly diminishing group of friends. And I'm one of them. Supposedly, I'll be one of the ones who will hang around for a while longer. Evelyn also ministers to a small group of surrogate daughters. Devoted to her only son, she missed that mother daughter relationship. I inherited Evelyn and my mother's other close friends when she died. Though Evelyn is the only one left in Mom's old group, Evelyn kept cultivating new groups over the years after Mom died. I have to laugh when I go out with Evelyn's crowd. I, too, am a senior now, though at the young end of the bunch.

So that summer evening, the kind of mid-June evening when summer is still balmy in Chicago, I met Blume, a friend of Evelyn, who always came up with another buddy, hidden away. Blume had raised her children in Skokie and now lives in one of the downtown high-rises. She and I were to wait at the Walgreen's on Michigan–Evelyn, an inveterate organizer, excelled at plan making–and then, together, with another friend coming with Evelyn from Hyde Park on the Jackson Park Express, we would all walk over to the concert together. While Blume and I stood at the corner waiting for the South Side contingent, we figured out who the other was and started a conversation. She asked me what I had been doing on the North Side, which was where I had been that afternoon.

"I went to a small gallery opening."

"Which gallery?"

I hesitated. The Jews in Skokie were always more traditional than my mother's friends on the South Side. But I didn't want to lie, just not in my nature.

"The Palestine Arts Gallery. It's actually very small. Pretty much the living room of a couple of artists. The exhibition is a preview of the show they are putting together for the commemoration of the Nakba next spring, you know..."

"I know. We call it the birth of our nation, and they call it the death of theirs. What we're doing to them. Such a shame. More than a shame. My niece is a journalist. She travels to the Middle East. She lived there while doing research for her doctorate. I can't talk to anyone about this, well, Evelyn, a few others, but, mostly, I keep my mouth shut. You can't say anything to the people here. I'm afraid to bring it up. AIPAC is so powerful. But not just them. They're like the pawns to power Jews have always been."

Analysis from a Jewish housewife. How I loved my mother's friends, and the friends of her friends. Some who had worked all day everyday inside and outside the house and never let their minds go dull. If only Leah could hear this. A Jewish woman from the suburbs, not your typical suburban housewife, but still. She, too, feels silenced. Guilty. I wished I could go home, go to bed, and wake up tomorrow morning, have an honest conversation with my sister about all of this. But, of course, that was not possible.

BITE OF THE BEAST

I, Emma Goldman, will admit that, alone, I do not pos-sess the means to mend the break between these two sis-ters. But maybe between the two of us, Gonzalez and I can make a difference. We have seen too many families break up over politics. They come wandering out of their lives, ready for some relief, confused about losing the people they loved the most. Beatrice needs to loosen up, quit the job of the sister sibling in charge. And Leah needs to give up her all consuming guilt and shame. But, wait, here comes Beatrice. She looks rested. At least, I still have the touch. That massage in the mountains worked.

The Passover after Sabra and Shatila. The massacres. That's when it started between Leah and me. The first Seder with Howard gone. Always it seems Israel and our family, we turn corners together. It struggles to its birth the same year I do, coming to its independence around when I start to crawl. Mom dies the year of the Six Day War, the year I begin to understand why Ida and Abe nev-er called themselves Zionists. Mitch and I get married in 1973, the year of the Yom Kippur War. I can always find a special private event to match up with the history of that place.

Oi vey! Rested she may be; transformed, she is not.

But, Emma, those massacres, happening just before Danny died and Mitch and I split up. And then Dad gone. Grief peeled away my ability to keep quiet. I couldn't keep myself from my outrage at Leah, the soon-to-be "born again, though never really had ever been before" Zionist. That Seder, sixteen unsweet years since the Occupation. The Seder of the start of the little war between my sister and me.

Leah and Eli had just bought their bungalow on Pearl Street near Santa Monica College. Painted blue like the buses, the college felt resort-like with the ocean and its uncomplicated beaches ten minutes away. Before the Seder of the beginning of our disagreements, Leah and I walked the soft, quiet streets while Randi and Michael kept their little cousin Raoul busy with a game of "house." When Michael realized that two-year-old Raoul would make the perfect baby, he knew Randi would promote him to Daddy. Only three minutes older, Randi took charge of "house" and most everything else.

So Leah and I walked, and we talked. We cried about Dad, and then we got to Mitch.

"Bicie, any chance of you two getting back together? For the children, I'm thinking."

"My dearest Leah, in a marriage out of which the bottom has dropped, do you think the nest remains comfortable for the babes on the perch?"

"Is it sex?"

"No. Sex is great. Of all the experiments, the one with Mitch proved to have the most successful results."

"Then, *what,* Bicie?"

"Me, Leah."

"What do you mean?"

"That's what I need to find out."

But my sister's concern for Randi and Michael only poked at my own. My precious ones. The miracle births.

Twins born on different days in separate years. Randi, first, of course, on my due date and New Year's Eve, the seconds ticking away to New Year's Day and Michael's official landing. I think that's why he makes such a big deal about time. Forced to look like he's a whole year younger than his twin sister, he vowed never to arrive late again. We didn't talk about Leah's "break" that much. After all, never the ambitious one, I did not question her decision to abandon the academic track. She could have gotten a plump position at Claremont College. Her dissertation adviser almost guaranteed it. An Americanist, she would fill a recently vacated slot and start the track for one of those coveted lifetime positions. But she bolted for the flea markets and polishing silver. I didn't know about her journals then. Why she started a kind of writing she could not stop. Had I known about those books she was building secretly, quietly, cautiously, and then hysterically, I might have tried breaking in. I might have tried remaining silent. I might have tried…anything else besides what I did.

That Seder we had our first real argument about Israel. Dad would have stopped it, but without him to hold us together, we fell apart. And then came the song problem. No matter Howard's disdain for organized religion, he managed to maintain his memory for Hebrew, which left all the Seders to follow vaguely empty. Our voices trailed in places he would have bolstered. Eventually, Raoul learned Hebrew and led us back, at least, to musical harmony, but now we sank into our multiple sorrows. And the start of our arguments.

Then it happened. Eli called me when we returned to Chicago.

"I'm worried about Leah."

"What do you mean?"

"She sits and stares out the window. She can't sleep. She reads to Raoul but doesn't do much else."

"Should I come out?"

We didn't trust therapists, so un-Jewish of us, but, desperate, I suggested Eli try to find someone for Leah to talk to.

"Well, let's wait. I just wanted you to know. An alert. Hopefully, it will pass."

It did. Leah plunged, then re-emerged a Zionist. And I started to see Paul.

How unoriginal of me to start dating a former professor. Shaheen, as I called him, in pure moments of tenderness, had introduced me to immigration law through the clinical program at De Paul. I fell in love with working on asylum cases, and I fell in love with him. Ten years older and divorced, with one daughter now in college, Paul Shaheen had lost his first wife, Palestinian like himself, to an aneurism and his second wife, Irish Catholic, to a short marriage that didn't fill the hole his beloved had left. Andrea, who had become seriously involved in analyzing everyone after she entered therapy following her own divorce, suggested my choice of Paul made a statement to Leah. I disagreed.

"First, of all, Leah would never see it that way. She knows me better than that. Second, his ethnicity would not bother her, only his politics, and I bother her enough with my own."

"But he backs up your position."

"Actually, we have different positions."

"What do you mean?"

"He thinks my support for a democratic, secular state isn't practical."

"And who would, my old friend?"

"Some of us hold out for it."

"Any Jews among you?"

"Some."

"Any Israelis?"

"Andrea, I doubt you'd want my lecture on Martin Buber and Judah Magnes, or Albert Einstein."

"*Einstein?*" Andrea couldn't hide her curiosity.

"Yes, he originally…"

But before I could continue, she cut me off.

"Listen, Bicie. I just don't get it. Your obsession with Israel, and all that."

For once, I decided on avoidance.

"Okay, so are you happy, Andrea, that I'm seeing someone?"

"Mixed."

"Mitch, right?"

"Of course. What do you think?"

Danny had a different point of view but did not disparage Andrea.

Beastie, you must get used to this. The Mitch fan club–of which I, too, remain a member– will endure. But I understand the need to explore alternatives, as does Emma. We approve of Paul.

Having their support bolstered me as Paul and I continued to see each other. You wouldn't call us an odd couple, just an odd relationship. Or relationships. About once a year or so, I did what Paul called "cheating on me with your ex-husband." It usually happened when something came up with Randi or Michael, mostly Michael, who had a much harder time with the split than Randi did. Mitch would come over so we could discuss what we should do, and then he'd ask for a glass of wine after we figured it out, and then he asked for sex after the glass of wine. We rationed it, almost like we knew we had to keep something alive, not for the kids, but for us. Sometimes I'd be over at Mitch's doing his taxes, and it would happen. Not often, just enough. Enough to know we weren't completely done. Paul never objected. Jealousy did not occupy much of a place in his brain. Besides, if he could have had one night with Rashida, he would have grabbed the chance. So we understood each other. The difference, I believe, is that he and Rashida would have stayed together until old age and a different kind of death parted them, but Mitch and I, or I, had a lot to work out.

Actually, Leah was thrilled when I told her about Paul. She worried that I would descend into the loneliness of single motherhood. I didn't have her looks, which she didn't bring up, but I also didn't have her ability to flirt, which she tried and failed to teach me. Amazingly, the flirting lessons started when she was ten, and I was 16. She saw I had no game, and always precocious, she had enough for both of us. Of course, she never strayed from Eli, but she could turn moments with strangers into subtle propositions. For example, one time we were walking out of a restaurant when Leah, offered a mildly provocative "May I take advantage?" to the man holding open the door for people walking in. His response? "Any time." He barely noticed me as I slid by behind my beautiful baby sister's movement through the door and the world. So, in truth, Leah expressed relief when I told her about Paul.

I think I had a crush on Paul all through law school, but I also know that it didn't drive me from Mitch. That came with its own cause and configuration. The need I had to walk through the world alone, unafraid, with a lover for back up but not for power up. Mitch didn't get that. Paul did. I think age had something to do with it. Temperament. History. Rashida, perhaps. I could live with the certain knowledge that she remained the love of his life, along with the steady trust that I meant a lot to him. Paul and I never lived together, but the relationship, starting out by accident, became much more than convenience.

Cheryl, still single, had invited me to a party in her new apartment near Lincoln Park. One of those people who hates parties, I dreaded it, but I knew I couldn't not show up. The kids were spending the night at Mitch's, so I didn't have to get a babysitter and had no excuse. I dressed as appropriately as I could, and then forced myself out of the house and into my car. I love the ride from Hyde Park along Lake Shore Drive. Mom used to call it the French Riviera— the lake, so vast it offers its bounty to four different states, and the parkland, so green you don't mind the snow and rain needed to produce it, and, on your left as you drive north, the architecture of the rich. Of course, you also pass some of the poorest neighborhoods in the city before you get downtown and start heading north, but the Drive shields you from all that.

Beastie, I don't know what to do with you. Not happy to stay thinking about the French Riviera, you need to bring in poverty and suffering? You can't enjoy a moment without re-

93

minding yourself that others don't have it so good. Please give yourself a sleeve of a second to relax.

Okay, Danny. You're right. I promise to enjoy the ride, and I'll try to enjoy the party, even. But what the hell is "the sleeve of a second"?

What keeps you warm in the cold. What you use for protection. I don't know, it sounded good. Humor me. And take your mind off of the downtrodden.

I took Danny's advice. But I never made it to the party. After looking for a place to park in the crowded streets around Cheryl's apartment, I finally found one. Never an expert in the art of parallel parking, I assessed my chances, and they looked about 50-50. So I took a deep breath while I pulled from my data base Mitch's fool proof instructions: "First, align your car with the car in front of you keeping as close to it as you can—without scraping it, Bicie!—next, carefully start backing up; finally, 'the magic moment', when the right front of your passenger door aligns with the left rear of the parked car in front, your guide, you cut your wheels, and then..."

And then I nearly ran into Paul. It usually takes two people off duty to make an accident happen. Think about all the catastrophes you have averted by watching out for your fellow drivers, and thank all of those who saved you from a scrape or two for repaying the favor when you needed it. Those times exist, of course, where nothing will save you, except luck, which, too, has its place in every story of survival.

Beatrice, once again please get on with the story. I think everyone would like to know how you and Paul finally got into bed.

No foreplay, Emma? No build up? I'd like to savor the moments of this memory, all history now.

All right, dear. Take your time.

So I started to pull into the space and nearly backed into a guy who had stepped into my blind spot, and then behind my car, as he ran to catch a ball for some kids on the street. Paul. We hadn't seen each other in several years, so after the initial shouting, "Are you trying to kill me, lady?" and "Why don't you look where you're going, mister?" and then the embarrassing, and exhilarating, recognition of each other, we talked for a good fifteen minutes before he reminded me I needed to finish parking my car. Somehow it all worked. I slid into the place, and when I emerged, trying to make it look like my triumph was no big thing, he asked me if I had time for a drink.

Now we're getting somewhere.

One drink did not lead to another, but it did lead to an invitation to Paul's place a few doors down from where I had finally managed to park my car. Once there, I called Cheryl and explained what had happened telling her I'd be by later, already figuring I'd be calling her in the morning to apologize for not showing up. Cheryl wouldn't mind. The point of the party in her mind was for singles to hook up. Divorced, never been married, never want to be married. But no widows, or widowers like Paul.

So my long simmering crush emerged from its semi-buried state to meet what seemed like mutual attraction. Who would have known? With visions of the French Riviera dancing in my head, I fell into the arms of Paul Shaheen. Contradictions. Complications. Consummation.

That morning, after my call to Cheryl, who expressed delight and no surprise that I hadn't shown up, Paul made breakfast for me, and then we talked, making the second awkward move from former student and professor to lovers. Later we would add colleagues and friends to our descriptors. He asked me about my practice, why I hadn't stayed in touch, how my kids dealt with the divorce. I told him about my dad's dying, about moving into immigration law, about building on the ruins of my high school Spanish in Mexico while Mitch kept the kids for a few months. I didn't tell him that I hadn't stayed in touch with him because I thought I might end up in the very spot I found myself that morning. He told me about his daughter enrolled at Barnard, about Kate, his second wife, who left him so she could live a life free from ghosts, and about how he had thought of me from time to time. I wanted to tell him that I had no problem with ghosts but decided to save it.

Good. A place of comfort, and similar interests. But be sure to keep your own thing, my dear.

Emma needn't have worried. While Paul kept his focus on immigrants from the Middle East, mostly Syria, Lebanon, and Palestine, I continued to grow my practice with people from Latin America, mostly Mexico. Language, more of a consideration than Emma's well-meaning feminist advice. Though, for a few years, we did merge our practices. The rent we saved and the bills we shared allowed us to take on more asylum cases.

That notion of outsider linked us, bound us, helped keep us together for longer than either of us would have predicted. We understood the feeling of not belonging, more temperament probably than history. We should have felt like we belonged. Both of us born here, each into thriving immigrant communities; each third generation, the first or second one to make it into the professions– from peddler or shopkeeper to doctor or lawyer. Sure, a call to social justice and a debt to our immigrant grand- parents kept us doing the work, but we also both under- stood that unmoored feeling.

At first, I believe Paul's came more from the loss of Rashida while mine tagged me at birth. He insisted his preceded Rashida, that she had only provided him brief respite for what, for him, also constituted a congenital condition. And so we gathered ourselves. And held each other up against the brutal times where hope, which we thought we'd never lose, nearly came unmoored itself.

The 1980s in the USA. Not a pretty time for former college radicals or left leaning professors. Not pretty for the poor and working classes. Not pretty for the idea of a democratic, secular state in Israel and Palestine. Even Paul disagreed with me on that one, at least then.

But I had an old college friend, Deborah Walinsky, who moved to San Francisco and joined an organization there called the Jewish Alliance Against Zionism or JAAZ, a small but committed crew. I went to one of their meet- ings once when I took the kids to California for a vacation before Mitch and I split up. I felt more at home at that little meeting as a Jew than I had any place else. Sure, some accused them of opportunism, using their Jewishness to support the heresy of a democratic, secular state, but they celebrated Passover together and protested the old anti-Semitism, against Jews, and the new anti-Semitism, against Arabs.

Then the year where everything changed–Howard died, Danny died, I left Mitch–the year just before Leah and I started our private little war, Deborah wrote about her group's silent vigil outside a San Francisco synagogue on Yom Kippur. That year, 1982, after Israel invaded Lebanon and allowed the massacres of Sabra and Shatila to take place. Deborah and her friends knew they were coming onto enemy territory by going to the upper middle-class, pro-Israel congregation. As they stood in line, handing out leaflets to anyone who would take one, Deborah said she'd never forget the look of grief on this one particular old man's face. Dressed in his Yom Kippur best–a tailored, beige suit, blue tie, and starched white shirt–he whispered to Deborah. "Such a pity. This killing. Such a pity." That image kept me going for a long time. He had to hide from his friends that he sympathized with the protest. How many more of him assembled there that night? How would we count them?

And then Deborah mailed me a book of her poems, which I showed to my mother's old book club friends when they wanted to add a poetry collection to their list. They chose her book, and Edith, Rosie's best friend, told me about taking it to the beauty shop one day. She read aloud Deborah's poem that mourned the loss of compassion among Jews forcing Palestinians into refugee camps. The old Jewish ladies there cheered. Those voices. That man. Those women. Evelyn's friend Blume. Why can't they emerge in the press, on the pulpit, at the privacy of my own Seder, in the company of my own beloved sister? Who says there's only one way to be a loyal Jew?

During that time the idea of going to the West Bank and to Gaza started to take hold in me. I needed to see the refugee camps. I needed to bring back evidence of the horror going on in my name. It started to nudge me, and once it began, I could not quiet it. But I never found the right time or the right way until, finally, the fall before the twins' fifteenth birthday, Deborah wrote to see if I had any interest in going that winter. Mitch, of course, saw Paul as the instigator.

I couldn't tell if it was politics or sexual jealousy. Usually, Mitch could handle my relationship with Paul. I think he knew the distance between us, marked by Paul's mourning Rashida and my personal *mishegoss,* prevented our situation from developing into something that would threaten the odd connection Mitch and I maintained. A bond owed only partially to the children. But this trip had him worried, not just for my safety for but for the safety of our post matrimonial extra legal promise to one another.

"Mitch, this has little to do with Paul. Sure, I'll see his family, but I'm doing this on my own. Deborah has contacts for me and a cousin I can stay with in Tel Aviv."

"Okay, Bea, but I never thought I'd see you, the grand anti-Zionist talking about going to Tel Aviv."

"Well, Mitch, I'll have easy passage that way."

"You said you'd never use your Jewishness as a cover for your politics."

"I'm not."

Mitch didn't know about what else, and who else, had started to needle me.

Well, finally, mija, *I get some credit and some action as one of the men in your life.*

Danny's challenge had startled me.

You simply cannot keep up this hating yourself, Bicie. Remember in college when I finally gave up and loved myself completely, without crime or sin or sorrow. Remember that day, well, night really. You toasted it, and me, but we never toasted you.

So, yes, I needed to witness the effects on the Palestinians of the atrocities committed by my Jewish people, but I also needed to witness the effects on me of years of silent anti-Semitism in the city of Chicago. Did I fight against the notion of a Jewish state because I believed in secularism and had little faith in nationalism? Or did I fight because I hated myself as a Jew? Of course, Emma led the charge against the charge of "self-hating Jew."

Meanwhile, Danny knew he had to use a ploy. I would return with stories of atrocity and hardship. I would witness and give braised beef to my argument. All that happened, but something else revealed itself: a salty wound I would finally have to cleanse. This he knew from the start, and, despite myself, I began to understand.

The kids had their own reactions. Randi had prematurely adopted Rosie's ways. "Why not? No matter what I say you're going to do it anyway." I had already become a good reader of Michael's non-verbal messages, since he wouldn't talk much on occasions like this. And what did I read in his *punim*, one of my favorites? A trace of fear, covered up—I continued to read—with mild anger, protection, and then indifference, which almost kept me from going.

I wished Michael could loosen himself of this burden and carry only his own sweet gifts into life, but motherly influence lasts only so long. Then the world steps in. So you need to get all you can inside your boys by the time they reach thirteen or so. It's a more leisurely stroll with daughters. You can miss some steps and make them up, but with your boys you need to stay awake, and, even then, you might lose them.

Beastie, this pronouncement makes you sound so self-assured. Will you consider that not everything can be explained? Will you leave the lectures to Emma?

I'm insulted, Gonzalez.

This should be good. I don't hear them talking to each other much.

Emma, do not take this as a criticism, though you have to admit we all can use some revisions if not then, then now, mi abuelita, *yes?*

What? You think we made mistakes?

I think we all made mistakes, Missus Goldman.

I'm nobody's missus, mister.

And then, Emma turned to me.

Some of us grow to this realm more slowly than others, Beatrice. But, whether your friend knows it or not, I have allowed for some self-reflection. We thought the bombers had their place. We thought wrong, but who knew in those days? We were just starting out. Some in your generation thought we were right, and perhaps the next one has a chance of moving on. Meanwhile, at some point, Danny's little Beastie will see what I never could have known, I hope. I do not put my faith in small acts of terror, but I do not put my faith in some kind of god either. And no one's a saint, not even Mr. Divine Comic.

Not even.

Gonzalez, are you mocking me?

Never.

All right, I think we'll move on now.

Yes, my dear.

On and up, bubelah.

So, with Paul's blessings, Deborah's connections, Mitch's misgivings, my children's mixed responses, Andrea and Cheryl's befuddlement, and to my sister's surprise, I flew to Israel. I left right after the kids' birthdays. We used the plural not just because of its accuracy but also because it gave them their separate days, months, years, like ordinary siblings. They could twin when they wanted to and claim their individual identities when they needed them.

On January 2, 1992, I boarded a plane in Chicago to begin the first chunk of a journey that would end up a day later, as the globe twirls, in Tel Aviv. A place, I used to think, only those American Jews committed to the Zionist cause would ever explore. When most everyone else lay snugly in bed, still recovering from hangovers or dreaming about New Year's makeovers, I stood staring, bleary-eyed, at the video monitor listing departures, wondering how I, a secular Jew with anti-Zionist leanings, could embark on such a journey. No *aliyah*–the right of return granted to all Jews, (on my list of protests, of course)–this brief sojourn, felt slightly absurd. What did I think I could accomplish?

Beastie, no matter what, you must let go of this guilty piece of religious ceremony, the plodding down the aisle on bloodied knees, the styling of the shirt with pricks upon it, the wounded forehead, the hands stabbed and weeping, ropes slapped against the back. Why people want to break skin, I'll never know. They think perhaps they will find the evil there and dig it out. But it's not the evil, which unfortunately remains a part of human circumstance. No, it's not the evil.

That, we must accept. It's what we do with it. Do you under-stand, mi pobrecita?

Whose lecturing now?

Indulge me.

When Danny turned philosophical on me, I wanted to scream. I wanted logic, argument, exposé. Hard facts. I had a lot of time to think on the plane flight. Just before we landed in Paris, I came to a conclusion. I wanted to dispense with all of the discussion and proclaim once and forever that I am not self-hating, that I am just "right." *So Jewish of you.* Then we touched down in Paris for a stop-over, and I began to doubt myself again. *So...Jewish, yes.*

THE PROMISE

And so we went to Israel. To Palestine. Leah and me. Beauty and Beastie. Sisters. Yes, dear reader, I took Leah with me on that trip. She would not know it until years later. Danny and Emma took their leave, and Leah filled my brain. She didn't speak. I just talked to her. You'll see.

1992, a year before Oslo, after the first *intifada* had subsided and the second one had not yet begun.

Deborah's cousin Shira meets me at the airport in Tel Aviv. I soon settle into the spare room, left vacant by a daughter enrolled in Hebrew University. Shira knows of my intentions to go to the West Bank and Gaza and makes clear to me that she does not approve, but she puts me in touch with one of her friends in Peace Now with connections to Jews on the far left of Israeli politics. She figures they might help me. She loves her cousin Deborah but has no taste for American Jews telling Israelis how to do their business. She only smiles and nods when I come home that first day with stories about how weird it feels for people to ask me directions in Hebrew, mistaking me for an Israeli. Like I belong here.

Small things, like noshing my way home with a bag of almonds from a street vendor. In Israel, it's a daily routine. This oral habit. Jews can't stop talking or eating, or writing a book, about whatever crosses their mind.

Leah, you would love how it feels. But, for me, something unexpected. Something unforeseen.

In between my wandering the streets of Tel Aviv, I start making phone calls to the contacts Shira's friend gives me. Paul and I had decided that, except for my visit with his cousin in Nablus, I would make this trip my own.

My second day in Israel, the initial euphoria of "coming home" subsides. I think of Paul when I visit Yafo, formerly an Arab city, now annexed to Tel Aviv. I can feel its Arabness. Only to the extent that vestiges of our Semitic past remain in Jewish culture do I feel connected there. Then a wave of gloom comes over me in Tel Aviv. It starts reminding me of Los Angeles, in general–the tacky modern architecture, the broad avenues, the sea, the usual balmy weather–and L.A.'s Fairfax District, in particular. Hebrew lettering on the stores and Jews everywhere you look. Perhaps seeing Jews in the role of dominant culture unsettles me. But I keep thinking that this won't last. *They won't let you stay in this position.* And the "they" is not the Arab world. So, as usual, the complications multiply. It feels like home. It does not feel like home. If it feels like home, that feeling cannot last. Just look at your past.

That's what I need you to understand, my sister, my sweet.

And, then, I get word that my contact in Gaza advises me not to visit.

"People are very angry about the threatened deportations. It's not a good time to come."

In response to the killing of a settler in Gaza in early January, the Israeli government has called for the deportation of twelve Palestinians. Deborah had predicted it might be hard to get to Gaza, so I don't press the woman and instead start calling my Jerusalem contacts. I will find a way to the West Bank, to a refugee camp.

Akiva Sofer, my first successful connection, agrees to see me the next day. So, on my third day in Israel, I begin my life as a commuter between Tel Aviv and Jerusalem. Each morning I take a taxi outside the apartment on Ibn Givrol to the bus station where I catch an express to the holy city, one step closer to the West Bank and the refugee camps.

In Akiva's small office with its sparse furnishings, a Rigoberto Menchu poster hangs on the wall. Huddled next to a small heater, Akiva turns it toward me. Although clearly distracted, she wants to help.

"It is a difficult time," she reminds me, "what with the deportations."

"I've heard," I tell her.

Akiva, an energetic woman who enjoys her cigarettes, had served in the Israeli army in 1948. Then, a self-described Marxist and Zionist, she now calls herself an anti-Zionist. I tell her I am looking for an escort to the West Bank. She asks me how courageous I am.

"You know," she says, "you can take a taxi at the Damascus Gate, just around the corner from here, and go yourself directly to Deheisha camp."

Trying to hide my anxiety, I respond as calmly as I can.

"But my friend Deborah insisted I not travel in the West Bank alone."

"Yes, yes," Akiva complies. "Let's see if we can find you someone."

Later when I go to Deheisha camp with an Israeli Jew, who speaks fluent Arabic and is well known and trusted by many families in Deheisha, I wonder at Akiva's suggestion. If I had tried going there on my own, and had managed to enter without trouble from Israeli soldiers, how would I have found people who spoke English willing to talk to me? Perhaps I fooled Akiva. Perhaps she mistook me for someone who belongs. Or someone brave.

Akiva gives me a directory of Palestinian and left-wing Israeli organizations. She suggests I try the Palestinian Writers Union. I reach a man who tells me he is Abu. Trying to convince him I'm someone he should help, I hear myself babbling about how I wanted to know about the relationship between poetry and the Palestinian struggle. He tells me to call back in an hour. When I do, he assures me: "I will prepare for you a poet." I wonder why I didn't just give him my lawyer and social justice credentials, but these people are writers, and something quietly tells me I need my sister with me.

Remember, Leah, how you revived poetry for me after several teachers had killed it. You even made me understand the inscrutable Emily Dickinson, not the easy pablum poems they put in our textbooks but the ones that keep you alive once you burrow into them. You showed me how your poet engaged in a broad and quiet struggle for her life.

Pleased that I have reached Abu, Akiva tells me she knows him.

"He comes from the African quarter. He was in prison for seventeen years; he speaks fluent Hebrew. He will probably introduce you to the poet Ghassan Awad who was tortured during administrative detention. You have made a good contact. Abu will help you."

I thank her for guidance and set out for the bus back to Tel Aviv.

On the way to the bus, I stop at Steimatzky's, the Israeli chain bookstore, where I find a nice translation of modern Arabic poetry, which, of course, includes Mahmoud Darwish. For Paul and Leah. And me. So I buy the anthology and then after I leave the bookstore, I discover the Ben Yehuda pedestrian mall filled with outdoor cafes. Settling into one of them for an espresso and a read, I begin to feel like myself, or at least how I like to think of myself–capable, resourceful. That way, I don't jump back on the bus and head for Shira's, where I might consider nursing my anxiety by the heater. Instead, the coffee and literature recharge me. Then I realize I have time to visit the Old City before I return to Tel Aviv.

You'd be proud of me, Leah. I do want to see the Wailing Wall, what they call in Israel the Western Wall.

After I get off the bus, I walk into the wrong entrance of the Jewish Quarter and immediately get lost. A young American Yeshiva student takes pity on me. He points me in the direction I need to go, and then on my way to the wall, I find a small courtyard, where some green pokes out from the still melting snowfall that had landed the day I did.

But once I make it to the wall, I feel the wave of alienation I had experienced in the De Gaulle Airport, waiting to transfer planes to Tel Aviv, when I witnessed a group of religious Jews making their daily prayers. Here at the wall, I see–lined up four or five rows deep–the *haradim*, the ultra-Orthodox Jews; men on one side, women on the other. Tourists cluster among and behind them.

As I approach the wall, a Lubivitcher woman begins a smooth, insistent attempt to win me over. Jews have never been missionaries; if someone wants to convert, a rabbi explains how they hunt us everywhere we go—the hard life of being chosen, and chased. If the hopeful persists, only then does the rabbi relent. Of course, Lubivitchers need to establish your Jewish credentials; their proselytizing involves more of a "passionately trying to save the fallen." Turning from the insistent woman, I offer her the "no thanks" half-smile I would give a Jehovah's Witness in the States, and focus on the wall.

And then I step up to the Arab side of this place. The rectangular Aqsa acts as prelude to the Dome of the Rock where light and color play with the magic of numbers and proportion. Gleaming mosaic tiles cover the walls, colorful rugs line the floors, carved designs adorn the ceilings, and the sacred mandala shapes appear everywhere, delighting both tourist and supplicant. Muslims believe that Muhammed rose from the rock in the center of the dome to God. Inside the mosque, women kneel, praying. The Dome of the Rock sits on the site of the first and second Jewish temples, so calling this space contested is, you could say, an understatement.

Even now, before the second *intifada*, with its proliferation of suicide bombers, which none of us will know about until later, tourists stay watchful. As we leave the Aqsa, a woman with a British accent takes the sound of bulldozers for gunshots. Then as soon as that fear fades, her husband shouts out, "They're throwing stones!" It just looks like boys playing, to me, so I don't pay attention to his warning. And then, sure enough, as I approach the boys, I see the harmless and melting toys they have fashioned out of the rare snowfall that excited everyone, including the pilot of our plane saying we have come at a propitious time.

So, bulldozers, Leah. One of the ways that Palestinians suffer is through home demolitions.

It's one of the topics I promised Mitch I would not bring up at Passover. But here we are. In the middle of it. The sounds of those bulldozers, a different kind of bomb. It's not just the homes of supposed terrorists that are demolished but homes built without permits, and there are lots of those because, well, *you* try to make it through the Israeli building permit bureaucracy if you're Palestinian. But then I realize this polemic will not bring Leah closer. Mitch is right.

I apologize, Leah. The demolitions are wrong, but I promise to pay attention to not just the greed but also the fear that drives them. I can't keep you at my side and not consider what you might say.

THE OTHER SIDE

The next morning, as I cross through the drafty, dingy interior of the Jerusalem bus station out into Yafo Street to hail a taxi, several drivers turn me down when I ask for a ride to East Jerusalem. Finally, one agrees to take me. *Perhaps he's Arab.* But soon I know differently.

"Why are you going there? It's not safe," he shouts at me. "What are you going to do there?"

"I'm going to see a friend," I blurt out. *Is he nuts, or is he right? Or is he just trying to get more money out of me?*

"I hate going there. I don't like it," he rationalizes when I complain about the inflated fare.

But he succeeds in putting me back on edge. *Who do I think I am? What do I think I can accomplish here?* Anxiety drives me into another space, where time speeds up, but then I pull whatever threatens me into perspective. I brush off the taxi driver's unpleasantness, step out of his vehicle and enter the building on Salah ed-Din Street— an even more barren place than the complex that houses Akiva's office, not far from here, on the border between East and West Jerusalem. As I knock on the half open door of *Al Haiat* Press and Publications Office, and then cautiously peer in, I see three men, who look back at me with suspicion. In my concern for arriving on time, I have come forty minutes early. After his initial surprise, the large man seated at a central desk, invites me to enter and introduces himself as Abu.

I repeat what I told him over the phone, but this time I start by saying I am Jewish.

Why? I don't know, Leah. Something about honesty. Clarity.

"You are *Jewish?*"

Surely, he has met sympathetic Jews before. After all, he knows Akiva. But maybe that taxi driver was right. What *am* I doing there? Then I compose myself.

"Yes, I am Jewish."

Starting to relax, I think perhaps he's just playing with me, testing me, teasing me. Danny always said I was a perfect foil. So I remind Abu he promised to introduce me to a poet. He says that "yes" he remembers and then he excuses himself to make a phone call. As he is hanging up the phone, he explains that the director of this office of the Palestinian Writers Union will come shortly. They offer me my first taste of Arabic coffee, flavored with cardamom and served in a tiny paper cup. Soon the director arrives. He introduces himself as Musa. One of the other men will translate for us. I can settle into my culturally privileged position that allows me to travel thousands of miles from home and be reasonably assured that someone will speak English. After we talk for a while, Musa says he will arrange a meeting with a poet for me at four o'clock the next day. And so the preliminaries conclude.

As I leave the office and take the stairs down, back into the East Jerusalem traffic below, I wonder how people will read me here. Tourist? Israeli? Which would make me safer? I wish Paul were with me. Then I notice some Israeli soldiers harassing two young Arab men. Instantly, I feel colonial, disgusted with the body that I bring here, the body of the conqueror. The IDF* ignores me; I present no threat to them. And Paul is safe back in Chicago.

When I return the following day, I learn that the poet Ghassan Awad–just as Akiva had predicted–will join Musa and me. Today my new translator, Saleh, jokes a bit and then offers me the customary coffee. I ask him about an article in *The Jerusalem Post*, the English language newspaper, reporting on Palestinian rejectionists, those who oppose the peace talks. The photo includes a man who looks to me like Abu.

Saleh nods, "Of course, we oppose the talks. They offer us small autonomy. We want our identity." Then he asks me how I found my way to their office. My explanation that Akiva assisted me satisfies him.

"You have come through safe channels."

"And, for me, *you* come through safe channels."

I notice a trace of disdain on his face. *What does this American have to worry about?* But he does not know about the taxi drivers, Andrea and Cheryl back home, or Shira back in Tel Aviv, who all think me crazy to try to visit the West Bank. He does not know about Leah at my side.

When Musa enters the room this time, I realize he reminds me of a friend from high school, Robert Levine, president of the math and chess clubs, and a secret poet I later found out. Today while talking a bit more about himself, Musa answers my questions about poetry and culture.

"We have been under four different occupations: Turkey, Britain, Jordan, and, now, Israel. Under this kind of continuous oppression, the occupier does his best

---

* Israeli Defense Forces

to destroy our cultural life. In addition to harassing us twenty-four hours a day, killing, deporting, arresting us, searching our houses and offices, bulldozing our houses, confiscating our land, closing colleges and universities, continuing to censor our magazines and newspapers, banning new books and other publications, putting curfews on villages and refugee camps, the occupier, whenever he can, prohibits us from conducting educational and cultural ceremonies, plays, seminars. Because of all this, because we have no power, we take our power by enlightening and educating our people through folksongs and stories, through poetry, to prove that we are still alive, that we still exist. In Ramallah, when there is a play, or some kind of cultural seminar, the seats fill up."

He pauses, sips his coffee, and then continues.

"Poets here write while the occupation hovers over their heads. The masses adore the poets and artists because we compose and create with true and genuine feelings. Language and song are the toys of our children."

At this point Ghassan Awad, the poet Musa has arranged for me to meet, arrives. I can see right away that he is a broad, confident man, less reserved than either Abu or Musa. All three of them have spent time in administrative detention. There's something about Ghassan that reminds me of Paul.

I don't know, Leah, why I need to make these connections with people I know. People back home. I guess I'm still grounding myself somehow in this place, on the other side, where I feel less at home but oddly not a stranger.

Skipping introductions, Ghassan moves quickly to answer my questions. He explains how the Israelis tortured him, treated him "like a dog," held him in isolation in a dirty cell with his hands continuously tied behind his back and a dirty sack pulled over his head.

"As much as I try to express how bad it was," he tells me, "I cannot."

But he seems eager also to answer my questions about the place of poetry in Palestinian culture.

"We would read to seven, eight hundred students at political events at Bethlehem University in the seventies..."

His gently gesturing hands start to hypnotize me. My mind wanders. I think about Leah again. I feel like a kind of imposter. I found my way to these writers by saying I wanted to hear about poetry in their culture. I took what she loves the most to come to talk to people she fears the most. I needed them to trust me, so I could hear first hand the treatment they experienced. I could have come as a lawyer. But I left those professional credentials at the door and slipped through with Leah's passport. Have I stolen her identity as a way to bring her along with me, to win our yearly Passover arguments? What kind of a fraud am I?

See, Leah, now you know. Now you understand.

I focus back. Ghassan cannot separate his talk about poetry from his talk about his imprisonments. He tells me about Ansar III, a detention center in the Negev, where other prisoners asked him to recite his poetry on national days of remembrance.

"Their love for poetry greater, it almost seemed, than we ourselves had for our own writing. Their discussions," he claims, "more intriguing than the best of literary critics."

I think about this beloved poet and how the Israelis treated him "like a dog."

"When you leave detention, you drag it with you, Beatrice. You brush it into your hair in the morning and roll it into your sheets at night. It never leaves you. The humiliation."

And then he lowered his eyes. This proud, handsome man, not broken but forever changed.

As the short winter day closes down, Ghassan offers to drive me to the bus station. We say our good-byes to the others and I my thanks, and then we take the stone stairs down and out of the building. As we make our way in his little car through the circuitous streets of Jerusalem, Ghassan continues to talk and, then, near the bus station, he asks me if I want to go for a beer.

So we end up talking for another hour at a little table in a place near the bus station, and then he settles into his question.

"So where does your interest in poetry come from? You say you are not a poet yourself. My little experience with American culture is that there is not a broad attraction to this art form except among poets themselves."

See, Leah, are you happy now that I brought you with me?

"You're right. My sister Leah is a poet and a teacher of poetry, and she introduced me to all of her favorites, including Emily Dickinson and Emma Lazarus. Leah is a traditionalist, but you should know that poetry is reaching broader audiences in the States now. There's a kind of revival. Leah says it's a bit like what Emily Dickinson said about witchcraft."

"And what was that?"

"*Witchcraft was hung, in History,*
But History and I
Find all the Witchcraft that we need
Around us, every Day–"

"An American who recites poetry, I'm impressed. And an American who talks about witchcraft…"

"Well, what Leah says is that poetry is like witchcraft. It's so powerful that no matter how hard repressive governments try to kill poets or try to kill poetry, it will spring back up."

"It sounds like you had a good teacher."

"Yes, Leah is a very good teacher, though she hasn't done it formally for a long time."

"It also sounds like you love your sister very much."

"I do, but something has come between us."

"What? A man?"

"No, no, nothing like that."

"Then what?"

"Your country."

"*My* country? Oh…she is a different kind of American Jew?"

"Yes, you could put it that way."

"And so you have come here to gather evidence to prove you are right."

"Not just with Leah."

"No, not just with your sister."

I'm starting to feel some tension. This man is in the middle of a struggle for his life, his people, his country, and I appear to have nothing much more on my mind than a struggle with my sister. It's so much more than that, but I can't seem to express the depth of the split in the Jew-

119

ish community. The fear and the rage on one side, and the anger and commitment on the other. And perhaps, even worse, the indifference among people like Andrea and Cheryl whom I love dearly and who, I have to admit, have many more fellow travelers than either Leah or I do. I want to tell Ghassan all of this. Something makes me think he would understand, but I feel like I did when I started keeping a diary at nine after I read *The Diary of Anne Frank*. What could I possibly say of any importance? My petty nice Jewish girl life, and all that.

"I came as a kind of witness..." I begin to sputter.

"Beatrice, you don't need to explain. You are here. When you go home, please tell people that I am a humanitarian writer. I ask my enemy to feel, to remember the love we all have for children."

He looks away and toward the bus station.

"It is time for you to go."

I get up first, and then he stands up, and motions that he will walk me to the bus. Once in line, I offer him my hand and my promise.

"I will tell."

"I know."

The next night back at Shira's we visit with her Aunt Dina and her cousins. When the talk turns to the *intifada*, Dina looks at me directly.

"They threw stones at us in Poland; they throw stones at us now. What's the difference?"

I think of Ghassan but don't respond out of respect for Shira. I decide not to "throw" his story at Dina but instead to find a way to a place where she and I might agree. She knows why I'm here, and I'm sure she's heard stories from the other side. I begin a conversation with her about the effects of trauma on children, raising the possibility that perhaps a country so full of survivors and their children might be overly susceptible to fear and paranoia. Shira, a psychologist, agrees.

"Some people drink or do drugs or both. Some people beat their partners. Some beat on themselves. Some live in chronic states of alert or panic."

This is where Shira and I can agree. But, I want to tell her, some come out the other side filling themselves with new longings, facing the evil the former victims have now begun to perpetuate. And others call those Jews traitors to their own people. If I were to say this out loud, Shira would be too polite to call me "traitor," but she would think it.

"Collective sociopathology. That's what war is."

Paul had his own ideas about how to fight injustice.

"War proves that you can turn anyone into a sociopath, or almost anyone. There are those who founder, who flee, who shoot themselves, who refuse one way or another. There are always those in every war, even the so-called good wars, Bea. And armed struggle? What we call defending your family, your home, your right to live free of torture, where is that line, beyond which your soul perishes?"

Akiva had participated in the armed struggle for the state of Israel, but she saw the line Paul talked about and crept back across it. She retreated, went into the ground, under the water, through the tunnel, and emerged clear, perhaps anxious but not afraid. I can only go so far with Shira. I wish I could tell her about Akiva and about Yael,

Akiva's friend. Yael Ben-Ivron spent time in jail. A Jew accused by other Jews for joining the other side.

I wish Leah, you could meet her. Shira, too.

And so, Yael's story. Her side, and mine.

"My family has lived in Palestine for five generations. My parents' friends included many Arab families. But my parents split when the war for independence came. My father signed on to fight. My mother, having just given birth to me, could not understand how their life-long Arab friends could become enemies. She loved being Jewish, but if it meant turning away from people she had grown up with, she could not comply. With everyone calling her crazy and a new baby to take care of, she started to break down. Then she turned over in bed one night, with me at her side, and wept, off and on until the morning.

"When the tears finished, she got out of bed, dressed herself and me, and left my grandmother's house in Hebron and traveled to Jerusalem where she got herself a job cleaning and cooking in the home of a well-off Jewish businessman. The family gave her a room where I could nap during the day. When I woke up, the family, especially their young six-year-old son, Aaron, would play with me. When I turned sixteen, Aaron made public to his family his love for me, and on my nineteenth birthday we married. My mother had taught both of us how to question the 'big people,' as she called them. That included Aaron's parents, her own family, my father, the Israeli government, anyone who went against the 'heart of love'."

Yael pauses briefly to compose herself, realizing she is telling me more than she had planned on.

"That is how my mother spoke. She danced at our wedding, and then five months later, just after I told her I was pregnant, she died. I wished I had asked her more about her 'heart of love'. I never knew if there had been anyone besides my father, but I think so. I also think she never got over the separation from her family. But she lived for me and approved of my husband. So she had done her job. Aaron's parents didn't mind that he spent so much time with us; it gave them more time for each other. Selfish people, they only objected when they saw where our beliefs sent us. The extreme side of the left."

And then the story I came for.

"We learned Arabic. We started a newspaper that predicted the *intifada*. We went to jail. We split up. Our children love us both deeply, but they have gone the other way. They serve faithfully in the army. No objections."

As Yael tells me her story, I think about what the "self-hater" name calling Jewish syndicate in the U.S. would say about her. This Jewish woman, daughter of another Jewish woman, who had grown up in this land, whose "promise" turned on itself, thinks like I do. Yael's mother did not hate herself as a Jew. She loved herself, and she loved this land, where once Jews and Arabs lived in peace. Yael, an Israeli, does not hate herself or her people. She just sees them as misguided. With no prophets in the land, or anywhere else, they don't know where to turn.

"The 1982 Lebanon war was a decisive moment," she continued. "It made clear that the destructive power of the Israeli government was very serious and that we had to be serious in countering it. Since the government wanted to destroy the Palestinian national movement, we decided to try to understand its goals, its development. Our first step was to learn Arabic."

Yael brushes aside my attempt to ask a question.

"In 1985, we started publishing, in Hebrew and Arabic, our newspaper. We brought to Israeli society word of the trade unions, women's organizations, the student movement, emerging in Palestinian life. In 1986, we established a joint board of Jews and Arabs, and, in 1987, we moved to bi-weekly publication in each language. We were the only paper to publish the photo of each martyr of the *intifada* with details of his or her life. In January 1988, one month after the *intifada* began, the State gave orders to shut down the paper. They accused us of having links to the DFLP.[*] Some professors and other liberals inside Israel and international human rights organizations, such as PEN, Amnesty International, and Journalists without Borders, defended us. Israeli liberals argued that the threat to freedom of speech could eventually spread to the entire society. Despite the protests, Israeli authorities officially closed the paper in February, but we continued to publish."

I think about the courage that took, how they must have known what would happen.

"That month the government began arresting the newspaper's journalists. One of us was tortured. A number of us received administrative detentions. Meanwhile, the police raided the paper's offices, confiscating addresses and phone numbers, ledgers, and other business papers. Shin Bet, the Israeli Security Service, interrogators tried to bully my friend and me into committing suicide when they had us in detention, and the police used our vulnerability as mothers against us, telling us lies about

---

[*] Democratic Front for the Liberation of Palestine

the welfare of our children. Two of us spent eighteen months in prison; one was imprisoned for two and a half years, with twelve months in complete isolation. I served nine months. The brutality of the Shin Bet, as it became nationally and internationally public, eventually turned into an embarrassment to the government."

But all of this had its costs. The love story of Yael and Aaron has ended, the fairy tale that Yael's mother created in her little room, finished.

"You know, I'll see Aaron give a speech at a demonstration, and I get those old feelings. We just can't live together. We fight all the time. I think we take our anger at the situation out on each other. We never learned to sort things through."

I envy them that they still share the active political struggle. Mitch has become too cynical for us to even have those kinds of conversations.

Then I ask Yael about the peace talks. Although she does not support the talks as currently constituted, she doesn't call herself a rejectionist. She argues that the Palestinians need to hold better cards. Israel has to make some substantial concessions in order to convince the world her intentions were not entirely self-serving. Yael points to the quotation from Malcolm X on the wall calendar: "I'm not going to sit at your table and watch you eat, with nothing on my plate, and call myself a diner. Sitting at the table doesn't make you a diner...You must be eating what's on the plate."

Yael identifies for me which segments of the Palestinian and Israeli community support the talks. The Popular Front and the Democratic Front have no faith in them.

The UNL[*] of the *intifada* is split. The Israeli Peace Movement, for the most part, is in. Those who accept the Zionist position, which sees Israel as a super power in the Middle East, think the talks are the answer everyone has been waiting for.

Then Yael looks at me with a flash of curiosity, the kind that drives people who are used to making other people uncomfortable, and makes me an offer.

"Listen, Beatrice, I'll take you to a demonstration this afternoon if you like. A protest against the deportations. You'll see the various parts of the pro-Palestinian movement there."

Grateful for the invitation, I agree to meet her back in the office in an hour. By now, I can easily find my way to the Damascus Gate—one of the seven-gated entrances to the Old City. Stopping at the stalls, I buy a small wallet for Michael and a pair of earrings for Randi. Although many Israelis think it's not safe for tourists in the Muslim Quarter, people appear friendly, enjoying the sunny day, warmer than earlier in the week. The sweep of the crowd gently moves me along, and that feeling of belonging oddly returns for a moment.

Once back at Koresh Street, I find Yael. She wants to use her car because she has other things to do after the demonstration. We're just a short distance to the East Jerusalem theater, where the demonstration is gathering. After we park, she tosses some Arab literature onto her dashboard, a way for people with yellow Israeli license plates to protect themselves and their vehicles in Arab towns and villages. A *kifiyeh* could also do the job, she

---

[*] United National Leadership

tells me. As we walk to the theater, Yael explains that in the mid-eighties it served as an active cultural center but now operates mostly as a meeting place. The demonstration will denounce the talks and support the rights of the threatened detainees.

Yael translates the banner strung across the stage: "Our response to the deportations of twelve freedom fighters is the stopping of the negotiations and the inclination of the *intifada*." I see Akiva and Musa and others I have met, who welcome me with nods or smiles. A television camera records the drama: Israeli soldiers posted around the theater and the wives of the detainees seated in the front row. Suddenly, a shower of leaflets fills the air. Yael explains that it's illegal to distribute this kind of political literature, but, since the source of the paper spray remains anonymous, the soldiers will arrest no one. Yael again translates for me: the leaflet is endorsed by the DFLP, the PFLP*, and Hamas. The secular socialists and the religious fundamentalists often find themselves in agreement.

After several speeches, with Yael continuing to translate for me, we leave because she has decided I should see the Women in Black weekly vigil. We say good-bye to her friends and leave by the side door. I later read in *The Jerusalem Post* that Yasser Arafat spoke to the rally from Tunis via live telephone. On our way to the vigil, Yael and I encounter a traffic jam caused by a police roadblock.

"They do this to drive people crazy, to interfere with normal daily life. It's psychological harassment."

By the time we finally get to the vigil, the band of women has started to break up. I tell Yael I've stood with

_____
* Popular Front for the Liberation of Palestine

Women in Black in Chicago, inspired, like so many others, by these women here in Israel, mostly Jewish but also Palestinian. They never could have imagined they'd ignite a worldwide movement against the Occupation.

Moved by the first *intifada,* they spoke out by remaining silent for an hour once a week, gathered together at a Jerusalem intersection, and then Tel Aviv, and then the world. Serbia, Spain, China. The Israeli Occupation and other unjust military moves. Big cities, usually, but even small towns. Little Half Moon Bay, a town on the Pacific Ocean–coastside, they call it–thirty minutes from San Francisco. Deborah pointed them out to me on a day we took off to do some sightseeing when I visited last year. Though I can't be a regular woman in black–too earnest for me–I admire them, wherever they came from. Using silence to break silence. Withstanding sneers and name-calling: "Whore! Bitch!"

Anyway, now Yael and I stand on the street, and after we get over the deflation of the missed connection, our talk turns from Women in Black to political strategies to mothering children in these times.

"It's affirming for me, Yael, to find Jews in Israel I can identify with politically, but I don't know that I'd have your courage."

"Well, one doesn't plan on getting thrown in jail."

"How did your kids take it?"

"It was tough. My daughter pretty much fell apart. Luckily, I have a sister-in-law who, though she objects to our politics, loves our children and us and would make a good candidate for sainthood. Without Basha, I don't know what we would have done. My daughter's much better now, probably stronger because of all of this. My son, typical male, played the stoic one, but the day I got out, and they all picked me up, I saw him brush a tear from his eye quicker than most people could blink. I don't think he saw me seeing him do that, which is just as well. It's hard to get him to open up. But I'm working on it. It goes, bit by bit…Look, Beatrice, I need to drive over to Hebrew University to drop off something for my daughter. You can get a bus there back to the main station."

"Thanks. That would be great. And thanks for everything today. I'll call you tonight to see if you have any luck finding me an escort to Deheisha."

Before we part at the bus stop, she gives me Jeffrey Eisenman's number.

"He was a Zionist before he went to jail, and he is still a Zionist. You should speak with people from different sides who oppose the occupation."

I promise her I will.

On my way to the station, I realize I have some time before I have to catch the bus back to Tel Aviv, so I decide to go to *Yad Vashem*–the holocaust memorial, located on the outskirts of Jerusalem.

Something for you Leah. And for me.

Soon I'm on a bus headed to a place far from the events at the El Hakawati Theater. Crowded with mid-afternoon shoppers and schoolchildren, the bus ends up in another traffic jam, so I fight boredom by studying my fellow passengers. I observe two schoolgirls, sleeping peacefully, their heads barely touching as they bend toward the space between them. An old tape from my own childhood starts rolling. The Anne Frank tape. The one my meeting with Ghassan got rolling in my head.

An aspiring writer at nine when I first read the *Diary*, I envied her skills and related to her crush on Peter. I tried my own diary but became disappointed at its obvious smallness. The boys I wrote about were not hiding from death camps, although the mother of one of them had concentration camp numbers tattooed on her arm. Once in a while, as an adult, I think about police pounding on my door. I guess at which neighbor might turn me in. But in America the police pound on the doors of blacks and Latinos, not Jews.

My mind keeps wandering. *The two girls, sleeping so peacefully–what if this were fifty years ago and they sat crowded on a train, on their way to a death camp? What if, instead of traveling to the holocaust memorial, I am traveling to the holocaust itself?* Then the bus starts up again, and the driver, who had attached his *yarmulke* to his hair with bobby pins, gives a shout of celebration to the driver of a bus beside us. *This country is so small. We all know each other here. We all have this shared history. We made it through.* And, so, my double life here starts to dig into itself, perhaps the influence of too many holocaust movies. I finally feel the Jewishness of the place.

Are you happy with me, Leah?

The bus stalls a second time at another traffic tie-up. This time a taxi driver jumps on the bus to get change from our driver. They exchange an early Sabbath greeting. With little crime on the streets, the bus drivers carry change for passengers and anyone else who might need it. I could walk the streets in Tel Aviv alone at night and not worry about getting harassed. But some women in their homes face beatings by their soldier husbands, the same men who stop and search Arabs. Signs at bus stations warn Israelis to beware of unattended packages. Women's purses are searched at grocery stores. At Tel Aviv University guards examine book bags.

The sun brightened patches of snow remind me of an unusually clear winter morning in Chicago many years ago on my way to the Art Institute on Michigan Avenue, not long after Mom had died. Something about such brightness, such illumination in the middle of winter, encourages a person to get through the cold. Entire religions have been built around signs in nature. Miracles–the sea parts, the bush burns. People tell stories about them, and paintings depict them.

During the time Rosie lived apart from Ida, on Wednesdays after school, she made the trip downtown from the orphanage and rode the escalators in The Fair department store where Ida worked, to pass the time until they could go for those visits at the Art Institute, open late on Wednesdays. They left The Fair, arms linked, and then after dinner at the Automat, they walked up the stairs and into the "palace of art"–my grandmother called it. My mother's stories of those visits under the high bright ceilings of Chicago's most prestigious institution travel with me each time I enter that place, almost in a state of worship.

At Yad Vashem I wander aimlessly through the grounds, the multiple dwellings and mounds, the stone and iron renderings, the art carefully placed. Then, I find them: the photos, the facts, the horrors piled up, documented, arranged systematically, relentlessly, the text that proclaims the first signs of blatant persecution of Jews in

Germany. *Barred from employment.* I think of similar restrictions against Palestinians.

I think about Shira's aunt, Dina, and what she told me about this army officer's lecture. He spoke about how he wept the first time he saw the home of a Palestinian bulldozed—a tactic the army uses, it says, to punish terrorists and their families. "But," he questioned—and Dina, whom Shira had described as being liberal years ago, seemed to agree with him completely—"what are we to do when our state has no capital punishment?"

I think about a discussion involving Israel, Eichmann, and capital punishment in my eighth grade religious school ethics class. The synagogue newsletter published my essay on the topic: "Should Adolph Eichmann be executed?" I argued that Israel should not make one exception to its stand against capital punishment—not even for a Nazi war criminal.

The illogic of the army officer's argument leaves me inconsolable. Because we cannot execute a person, we can bulldoze his home, without any trial? What happens when a moral code becomes so twisted that in order to defend it, one must stand it on its head? Israel made an exception for Eichmann and killed him, but at least he had a trial. Many Palestinians do not even get one, and their crimes, *if* they have committed them, cannot begin to reach the pile of Eichmann's. Sometimes the homes of accused are destroyed; sometimes they are simply shot in cold blood on the street.

Leah, how I wish you were here with me now. We'd argue. We'd cry. We'd make up and argue again. The lost sisters, talking again.

At Sabbath dinner at Dina's, I decide not to tell the family about my trip the next day to Deheisha, a refugee camp on the West Bank–yes, Yael has found an escort for me. I begin to connect with Dina's cousin, Chanah whose beautifully aged face, diminutive body, and cigarette smoking remind me of an old intellectual who has lived long enough to see her youthful ideas triumph, hold, and then give way to new, untried, contentious systems. I think of my grandparents' old, dear friend, Olga, wife of Maximoff. I don't know Chanah's politics, but I think she is on to me.

She has quickly eliminated all the other possibilities for my trip to Israel and has landed on my true purpose here. She tenderly fixes her eyes on me as she presses into my hand a piece of paper on which she has written the name of the exact corner to catch the taxi, the *sharoot*, that I would need to take to get to Jerusalem the next morning, since the buses would not be running due to Sabbath. While everyone else has been arguing, trying to decide where the taxi stops, Chanah silently writes the answer for me on the slip of paper.

The next morning I catch the bus outside Shira's apartment and ride it to the corner that Chanah had carefully printed on the piece of paper. Sure enough, the *sharoot* is waiting. The cold snap has passed. I take off my long, heavy coat and settle in for the ride to Jerusalem.

Once there, I make my way to the King David Hotel, near the Cinemateque, where my escort, Yael's friend Rebecca Goldstein, plans to meet me. Arriving early, I wander around the hotel's elegant lobby, thinking of the Jewish Americans who have stayed here during visits to the Promised Land, the place they have sent their money and lavished with their dreams of safety and survival. Rebecca's father, an American born Jew, made the ultimate investment and commitment: *aliyah*. He permanently "returned" to the Holy Land, the right of every Jew under Israeli law. Rebecca and her two siblings, all born in Israel to an Israeli mother, live comfortably in Tel Aviv. In her late twenties, dressed in casual, hip clothes, Rebecca could easily pass for a graduate student at an American university, a role she once played at Harvard. We find each other on the street outside the Cinemateque. She knows me right away. Yael described me well, or maybe I don't look so much like I belong, after all.

"Beatrice?"

"Rebecca?"

At last, I will make my way into the West Bank, and my guide, with the same last name as an elementary school friend, is here.

Before we get started on our trip, Rebecca wants to give me some background information. We sit at a table, drinking coffee, in a café inside the theater with an expansive view of Mount Zion. When I comment on the beauty, Rebecca jokes, "That's the advantage of being the conquerors. You get the best views."

Rebecca's story pulls me in. Committed to the struggle for Palestinian independence, she acquired fluency in Arabic, so she could travel in and out of Deheisha on a regular basis. She started visiting the camp because of her political work, and then she began to gather information for her dissertation in anthropology at Hebrew University, where she would analyze how the constant absence of young men–due to migration for work in the Gulf States and continual imprisonment or detention–affects family life at the camp.

"Virtually every youth you will see," Rebecca tells me, "has been in prison, many of them imprisoned before the *intifada* and some held for years--five, eleven, fifteen. Since the *intifada*, people have gone for shorter periods but are arrested more frequently. Commonly, they serve six month terms of administrative detention."

Rebecca continues by giving me some of the facts about the refugee camps.

"There are twenty-eight camps on the West Bank, a total of fifty in the Middle East, including Gaza, Lebanon, Syria, and Jordan, with populations ranging from 1,000 to 50,000. After the 1948 war, hundreds of thousands of Palestinians left Israel. Not all of them became refugees, but a high percentage of them did. Jordan is the only country where they got citizenship. Today 750,000 to 800,000 people live in Gaza–a place that is only about 4 miles wide and 25 miles long. Gaza is the world's most densely populated area. In a way it is one huge camp, even the urban centers. Conditions there are the worst. Jabalia Camp in Gaza is where the *intifada* started. The West Bank refugees are a rather small percentage of the refugee population."

Rebecca patiently pauses while I scribble some notes. Though deeply confident about her work, she is a generation younger, which creates more of a distance between us than I felt with Yael. Also, her reserve triggers my own insecurity, so our conversation starts out a bit formal. She lectures, I occasionally interrupt for questions, and then she continues. But her slight impatience worries me. Does she trust me? Am I worth the risk of taking a stranger into the camp? The main concern always the IDF. But also will I do something to damage her carefully built trust with her Palestinian connections? I try to remain as respectful as I can, showing her I understand the generosity of her escort.

"People in the camps are unarmed," she continues, quietly forceful, but neither aggressive nor arrogant despite her obvious disgust over her government's practices. "They have no means of self-government. But the refugee camps have been in the lead of the *intifada*. During the *intifada* the number of arrests and administrative detentions has been high. Curfew has been imposed often, sometimes for as long as two to three weeks. Of course, the longest was during the Gulf War. During curfews, people cannot go to work or visit friends. Soldiers are allowed to shoot to kill if someone breaks curfew. There is a high military presence; the degree of surveillance and control has increased dramatically since the *intifada*."

Then Rebecca talks about Ansar III–the detention camp known by the Israelis as Ketziot–which I had already heard a little about from Ghassan who had spent time there. Rebecca provides more details.

"It's located in a desolate place in the middle of the desert, 40 kilometers south of Be'er Sheva, it houses around 7,000 prisoners. The weather is hot, dry, brutal. Prisoners are not allowed to have any visitors, and books and writing materials were initially prohibited. Finally, due to protests by left wing groups in Israel and international delegations, prisoners can now conduct study groups, which helps to keep up prisoner morale."

I ask her how her professors at Hebrew University deal with her obviously politically motivated dissertation topic.

"It's a fight, she quickly answers, "but I take the struggle for granted. I expect it."

We have finished our coffee now. Rebecca pays for both of us and wishes the man behind the coffee bar a good Sabbath. Once outside on Hebron Road, she hails a taxi going into the West Bank.

When we arrive at Deheisha, Rebecca preps me.

"Just act like you know where you are going. Follow my lead. Do not look bewildered or lost. The IDF may spring out at us at any moment. Be ready for that. Do not act alarmed or shocked. Do not act afraid."

The entrance to the camp is small. Inside, sparse vegetation, narrow streets, and grim cement structures blur into an oppressive gray. Stones and broken bricks obstruct passageways. We step over the open sewer. Rebecca talks while we walk.

"There is virtually no work in the camps, so people are forced to become daily laborers in Israel; some men work in the Gulf States, or Jordan and Egypt. Generally, the people live at a subsistence level, dependent on wage labor. There are a few small shops in the camps. People living in the towns and villages suffer far less from unemployment and violence. The villages at least have some land for agriculture."

We stop first at the home of one of Rebecca's friends, Ibrahim, but do not find him at home, so we talk briefly to his wife and then go up to the roof where we find his mother drinking tea and resting on a broken wooden chair supported by a cement block. The constant drone of traffic from the highway outside the camp presents only a minor distraction compared to the IDF tents visible from our perch.

On each roof sits a water container, and, on some of them, television antennas announce the modern world. Laundry drying in the welcome sun speaks of another. One of Ibrahim's sisters brings us tea. Like her sister-in-law, she wears synthetic stretch pants and a sweater. Her mother wears a scarf and a traditional garment of dark blue velvet with a machine embroidered flower design. The map on the face of Ismael's mother traces years of sorrow and loss. A widow for many years, she has eleven children. She used to work as a maid in public institutions, but now, too sick for heavy labor, she depends on her oldest son, who works in Saudi Arabia.

After we say good-bye to the women in Ibrahim's family, we walk the short distance to the home of a young martyr. That day the bereaved family will celebrate the double engagements of their twin sons.

"You are lucky, Beatrice. You got good weather today, and you will see a traditional celebration. There have been very few of these since the *intifada* began. Perhaps this is a renewal."

The family welcomes us warmly with typical Palestinian hospitality. We drink tea with milk and sugar, on the porch of the two-story house. Rebecca later tells me that some people have been able to build onto the cement block huts originally provided by UNWRA.[*] From the income sent to them by sons working in the Gulf States,

---

[*] United Nations Relief and Works Agency

they construct larger dwellings, relatively bare but much more commodious than the original structures. The family invites us inside where they proudly display pictures of their dead son.

"He was the brightest, the most talented," Rebecca whispers.

Rebecca points out the boy's drawings on a shelf. The family insists that we join them at the celebrations, but Rebecca resists because she has plans to see Omar, her friend and a respected hero in the camp.

Unfortunately, at Omar's house, we hear that he has already left for the festivities. Though visibly disappointed, Rebecca gives in to the ambience of the day, so we walk with the growing crowd to the house of the first fiancée. On the way there we encounter the IDF. Just as Rebecca has predicted, they jump out, seemingly from nowhere. As we move out of their way, I allow myself a backward glance and record the fearful eyes of one of the young soldiers, a Jewish boy wearing glasses.

Leah, most of them don't look afraid. Some of them walk like princes to the manor born, when actually they have stolen the manor. But their shame, I see their shame. Its cover, a shout or a shove or much worse.

So we arrive at the home of the first party, where all the women are gathered on a patio and the men mingling outside. When the woman's betrothed enters the patio, he adorns her with jewelry, and completes the ritual by placing a pearl necklace around the crown of her head, as if she were a princess.

"Jewish American princess!" Remember, Leah, when that neighbor made you realize it was no compliment. But what

devoted family would not want each child to feel precious,
prince and princess, bejeweled and beloved. A fairy tale. A
fable. Who has the riches, the land, and who does not.

At the next bride-to-be's house, again the women remain separate from the men. But with little room for us in
the crowded area where the women gather, Rebecca leads
me up to the roof where the men stand around, smoking
and talking. When we finally catch up with Omar, once
he makes his way up there, Rebecca reminds him he had
promised to meet with her today. He explains that he has
to stay for a short while more. As a popular leader, he
must put in his time at this event. People greet him with
respect, deference almost. Like Chanah, he has a kind of
intellectual energy and enjoys his cigarette as he speaks.
His gentle teasing manner reminds me of Howard. Clearly
accustomed to his charm working, Omar makes a promise to meet us back at his house before too long. We take
the long way back to Omar's house, while Rebecca guides
me through what I see.

"Minimal provisions of UNRWA. An antiquated sewer
system. Narrow and bumpy streets. Cinder block homes."

We pick through areas of slush, remnants of the recent snow, as we walk. Eventually we get to an area where
people do not know Rebecca. Up until then, I have felt
safe, confident as I hurried along with my self-assured
guide. Now I become a bit anxious, but Rebecca greets
the strangers in Arabic, turning them into friends.

As we turn the corner of one of the narrow streets, a
man waves us over. I guess that Rebecca knows him, but
later find out he just wanted to welcome us and share his
good news. When we enter his tiny house with few fur-

nishings, he introduces us to his wife who had given birth to a baby on the day I arrived in Tel Aviv, during the heavy snowfall. We admire the infant bundled in blankets, congratulate its mother, and then go outside to sit in the sun and sip the coffee and nibble the chocolates the family's young daughter delivers to us. Eventually, Rebecca makes polite good-byes for both of us as we head for Omar's.

From the first cup of tea I had with the journalists in East Jerusalem to this spontaneous celebration, the gracious welcomes that Palestinians practice go beyond the customary question "Would you like something to drink?" offered to the generic guest in the United States. Other Americans have remarked on this, so I'm not romanticizing these small moments. But I don't know if it's specifically Palestinian or something left over from a time when the traveler at your door really was weary. I remember a trip to the rural parts of North Dakota with a friend who grew up on a farm there. We had been at a conference in Fargo, and I went along as she visited her large family. At every farmhouse plates of ham, turkey, cheese, and rolls, along with pickles and tomatoes and, sometimes, cooked sausage, appeared soon after we did. Is it the bounty shared—no matter how massive or meager—the weary traveler comforted, or the sign that we are not enemies?

On our way to Omar's, Rebecca gives me some of his history. Born in Deheisha thirty-six years ago and imprisoned for eleven of them, he married a much younger woman because by the time of his release all the women in his age group had already married. He also missed out on college, medical school. Rebecca quiets a bit as we approach Omar's house. But when we arrive there, we find out that she must be patient for just a bit longer. Since he hasn't gotten there yet, we speak with his wife, Amal, and her brother, Muhammed.

Amal speaks fluent English. She tells me that she uses her degree in mathematics from Bethlehem University to prepare young students for the high school matriculation exams. Despite the intermittent closings of schools and universities by the Israelis, the Palestinian people have remained dedicated to books and scholarship. The obvious pride in her "How do you like my country?" stays with me. It obliterates the grim surroundings she lives in.

I think for a moment about how diaspora people turn song, poetry, story and conversation into homes they carry with them. Forced into exile, they dwell in language. But when Amal asks me about her country, I know she means the land. *That* was where she located her wealth. So should Jews abandon it? Is Grace Paley right?

Paley, my favorite Jewish writer, one of my favorite writers, period, claims that Jews should operate like some kind of conscience for the world. I love how she puts it, saying that we should remain "a remnant in the basement of world affairs" or a "splinter in the toe of civilization." Only an American Jew like me would ask such questions. Israeli Jews, even anti-Zionist Israeli Jews, do not have the luxury to consider them. This place is their home now. Rather than asking whether to leave here, they must figure out how to *live* here. With other people who also love this land.

Then Amal's brother, Muhammed, enters the room and immediately challenges me.

"Why have you come here?"

I try to explain the need for people in the U.S. to see the effects of our policies up close, the need for me as a Jew to continue to speak out. I mumble something about Jewish self-hatred.

"I don't hate Jews from America. I'm only against the Israelis who have taken my land."

Gradually, the air loosens around us.

"Well," he jokes, "the Palestinians go to Washington, and the American comes to Palestine."

As he smiles, I wonder about his vague reference to the peace talks and what he thinks of them.

Amal and Omar have three children, a four-year-old boy, an 18-month-old girl, and a one month-old-baby. Later, on the way back to Jerusalem, Rebecca tells me that Amal, a brilliant woman, in another place could fulfill her promise. But not here.

While Amal, Muhammed and I talk, Rebecca has her conversation with Omar. Then Muhammed and a friend give us a ride to the taxi that will take us back to Jerusalem. Once we get out to the main road, we find ourselves behind a truck full of soldiers, their guns pointing out at us. The car slows down, and our conversation stalls.

So, Leah, one day I'm in Chicago and a few days later in a car driving around Deheisha behind a truckload of Israeli soldiers. Who would have thought? Or dreamt? Or watched?

Back in Jerusalem, before we part, I ask Rebecca more directly about the peace talks. I tell her about my meeting with the Palestinian writers, my talk with Yael and how they hold little hope for the talks. Rebecca tells me that Omar and his friends support the talks, that a Deheisha resident who spent fifteen years in prison, had joined an advisory group for the Palestinian delegation. But somehow I feel that if I lived here, I would end up with Yael and her friends. The fantasy of talks when so much has been removed from the table does leave people hungry, and broken-hearted. I admire Rebecca and Omar's hope and persistence. I wish I could share it.

I'm sorry, Leah.

Meanwhile, I'd forgotten about my other attempts at getting into the West Bank, but someone else has been hard at work. That night, when I get home, Shira, greets me with a shout.

"Success! My friend from the kibbutz has arranged a guide for you to the West Bank. Ali works in the Palestinian non-violence movement, and he has promised to take you to a West Bank village. On the way, you will stop at Ramallah and Nablus. Isn't this good news? Just what you wanted."

Though grateful for Shira's coming through for me, I can't feel as excited about this victory. My day with people forced to give up most of their dreams and to squeeze other ones into tiny bottles they could measure out a drop at a time has sobered me up. Amal should be a math professor at a university and Omar, a physician tending to his people's bodies as well as their minds. But I thank Shira as graciously as I can. After all, she seems to have started to buy into the purpose of my trip.

And so I call Ali in Jerusalem. Over a scratchy connection, we make our plans. Since we agree to meet there early Monday morning, I decide to treat myself to an overnight stay in East Jerusalem at the American Colony Hotel, recommended by Shira.

When I enter the hotel lobby on Sunday, I see that this former home of a Turkish pasha still bears traces of the sweet life lived by royalty and colonials at the expense of others: mosaic covered walls, intricately painted ceilings, and impressive gardens, all of which compensates for the current draftiness and lack of hot water. Skipping the lavish buffet breakfast in the morning, I take my rich, dark coffee into the lobby while I wait for Ali to arrive.

When Ali enters the lobby a half hour later, he doesn't seem to want to leave right away, so he sits down and we talk for a while before getting up to go. Maybe he is testing me. I am getting used to this. Before long, his relaxed, joking manner eases my general nervousness and perhaps signals his approval, until we get into his car and he politely orders me to remove my sunglasses.

"They make you look more Israeli. I have yellow plates. We have to be careful."

"Of course."

We have yellow Israeli plates, and we're traveling into the West Bank. It's better if I don't look Israeli. Just when I was getting an oddly strange good feeling about those Jewish Israelis taking me for one of them, asking me for directions in Hebrew. Was it a feeling of belonging or just relief at not being taken for a tourist? And now it's better again not to look so Jewish.

For different reasons than when we were growing up in Chicago, Leah.

I think back to a day when Abe picked me up at school, probably in the third grade.

"You're ashamed of your greenhorn grandfather."

"No, Grandpa! I'm not ashamed."

But I *was* ashamed and horrified that he knew it. Ashamed because he looked like the Jewish immigrant paperhanger that he was. Ashamed of myself for being ashamed of him, when I adored him. Now I am ashamed of what my people are doing in this country, but I am not ashamed to be a Jew. I am finally proud to be who I am. Proud of Abe, and Ida, and Olga, and proud of the Jews who stand up against the crimes that other Jews are committing, most because they are afraid, some because they are simply criminals.

Is that what hurts you Leah, that I call our people criminals? Or are the crimes what disturb you?

I look over to Ali, from my passenger seat, as he continues to talk. He likes to talk. He talks about how he refuses revenge. He talks about reading Gandhi and Mandela and how he tries to reconcile Mandela's move from nonviolent resistance to armed struggle. He looks Jewish and feels so Jewish to me. Then I remember a conversation with an Iraqi Arab, one of Paul's clients. Hakim worked at a restaurant, and he was maligning his Palestinian boss.

"What you're saying reminds me of how I've heard people all my life talk about Jews, Hakim."

"It appears, Bea, that you don't know that people call Palestinians 'the Jews of the Arab world'. They are better educated. They are the merchants. They are, in fact, your cousins."

So, this time, with my cousin Ali, I travel into the West Bank.

With our final destinations Nablus and a nearby village in the northern part of the West Bank, we stop first in

Ramallah. On its outskirts I notice relatively large homes and remember that before the occupation Ramallah had served as a resort area. Ali has some business with a small graphics company where it turns out the people know Deborah and her friends who had painted a mural with a group of Palestinians. I begin to get a feel for the tight connections that pull together this world I have entered. Sometimes no degrees of separation, other times two or three at the most.

Ali's caution resurfaces when we leave the shop and the tense streets fill with people. A strike has been called, one of the main strategies of the *intifada*. Ali places his "Library on Wheels" sign in English and Arabic on the dashboard, a simple and protective gesture that indicates, despite his yellow Israeli plates, he comes in peace. All day when we pass through IDF checkpoints, Ali tosses his Arabic sign into the back seat and sails through on the strength of his yellow plates. I can't think of a more literal example of code switching than the dashboard game people play. I think back to Yael putting Arab literature onto hers when we went to the demonstration in East Jerusalem. And when Ali and I get to Nablus, he switches us into a car with local plates. Now we are completely legitimate. Ali relaxes, and so do I.

On the way to Nablus, he tells me about his car being stoned while escorting a Norwegian woman to a refugee camp. As he speaks, I start to notice the clusters of white houses with red-tiled roofs. Settler homes. Ali patiently explains how he lost some land, arbitrarily "confiscated" by the Israeli government. "I won't be bitter," he says, "but it's hard not to be angry." When a child is slain, he encourages the building of a park in the child's memory. Revenge does not interest him. He has his limits, however. "In this car," he jokes, "no smoking and no settlers. If I see one on the road, I won't pick him up."

When we arrive in Nablus, we immediately go to the home of an active member of the Women's Committee for Social Work. With a branch in the nearby Balata refugee camp, the committee works in villages and towns as well as in other camps. Alena, who wears a traditional scarf, does not call herself a feminist but works for the improvement of women's lives in more traditional ways. She explains that all four Palestinian women's committees, each from different political viewpoints, supports the *intifada*. She belongs to the only non-socialist group.

The Women's Committee seeks to preserve traditions—folklore, songs, dress—to raise the educational level of women, and to help them gain practical skills. They train women to sew and embroider traditional clothes and have established cooperatives that sell handicrafts and traditional clothes in local shops, especially important since the *intifada's* boycott of Israeli goods.** The cooperatives farm land and raise chickens and goats. The committee helps women if their husbands have been imprisoned or martyred. To establish relations with Israeli Jews, they have met and gone to demonstrations with Peace Now and Women in Black.

Her friend, Fatima, a teacher and administrator in the kindergarten in the village of Sebastiya, arrives, and soon is talking enthusiastically about her school. Their committee worked hard at setting up kindergartens in camps

---

* Boycotts, strikes, and stone throwing marked the first *intifada*. Suicide bombings did not appear as a systematic strategy until the second *intifada*.

and villages. When she offers to show the school to me while Ali takes care of some business in Nablus, I eagerly accept the invitation.

You would like Fatima, Leah. She reminds me of Mom. That energy. The love for life no matter what sorrow might bring her.

On the short drive from Nablus to Sebastiya, the hilly countryside alternates between patches of white stone and green vegetation. Inside the village we park along one of the narrow, winding streets near the school. Once there, a third woman, Amatallah, the head of the Sebastiya Women's Committee, shows us around. She explains how they have divided the old stone building into two classrooms and sectioned them off into learning centers, including a mock kitchen and doctor's office. Outside in the courtyard, murals decorate the walls.

Later, Amatallah takes us to the nearby Roman ruins. And, finally, we come to what remains of a temple. Here she explains that the Israelis had robbed the ruins of their former beauty and riches. A round piece of marble stone, half buried in the ground, marks the entrance to a room, the only remnant of a mosaic floor. I think of fragments like these at the British Museum, the Oriental Institute in Chicago; the potential for atonement vast.

"You will want your camera now," Amatallah reminds me.

When I tell her I have no film left, she sweeps aside my regret, "That means you will have to return here someday for your photos."

I appreciate her warmth, but I consider instead perhaps how the spirit of that place resists my intrusion. I think about how these former monuments to power, in their broken down state, overgrown with grass and trees, allow the distant empire to give way to the mystery of time passing. We visit what's left of a group of pillars where the Roman Empire hanged men who refused military service. I think about Jeffrey Eisenman, the American Jew and Zionist now married to an Israeli and living in Jerusalem, who refused to serve in the West Bank. Yael told me I should talk to him. She respects him, though his Zionism didn't fit with her beliefs. I appreciate how she didn't disavow him or belittle him.

Jeff spent twenty-one days in the Jericho jail for refusing to serve in the Occupied Territories. Eventually, the army threw him out. Had he been younger, he would have suffered endless bouts with prison, a ruined career and life, perhaps. Instead he wrote a book about his time in jail. He found his voice protesting the injustice of his adopted and beloved country. He then started to investigate and write about torture by the Israeli General Security Services, the GSS. He bends his head in sorrow when I finally meet him and he tells me about this work. "What have we become?"

So he resists, yet refuses to bury his Zionism. He will stay in Israel with his wife, an artist, and children and friends, the community they have built with people like Yael and Akiva in a land, I now fully realize, they all love.

You would also like Jeff, Leah, like you, a Zionist. Like you, a troubled mind. Like you, like you.

So next we visit the ruins of a Roman amphitheater. Slaves, prisoners of war, criminals, Christians condemned to death, gladiators all, spent their final moments giving perverse pleasure to large crowds. I think of Jews and Palestinians pitted against each other by larger empires. As they wrestle for this land, who watches, smacking their lips like the spectators at this amphitheater?

As Alena, Fatima, Amatallah and I continue our walk, Amatallah tells me about her life here. She loves spending time on this hilltop with the children, playing music on her cassette, but she complains of the settler houses disturbing the view. She talks about how in the early days of the *intifada*, skirmishes with soldiers took place nearby. I start to see how in this place no greenery, surviving stone, or meditative moment can remain innocent.

I find it hard to leave the peaceful hill, but I know I don't want to miss the next part of the plan for the day, when my lived life in Chicago will meet up with my traveling life on the West Bank. Paul wanted me to meet the son of his grandfather's sister, a man named Moussa Hanania.

Ali had shouted out in disbelief when I gave him Paul's cousin's name during our first phone call.

"Beatrice, you have fallen into the right hands. This man is an old professor of mine. It will be easy for me to prepare a visit with him."

So, eventually, the four of us women on the hill reach the place where we'd begun. We climb back into the small car and drive the short distance back to the village, where we drop off Amatallah, and then, Alena, Fatima, and I drive to Nablus to meet up with Ali. Since Fatima had also studied with Dr. Hanania, she decides to make the visit with us while Alena returns to her home where we will later share a meal.

Before we leave Amatallah in the village, she wants me to visit her home.

"Next time," I say, seriously wondering where my quick confidence came from.

For the first days of my trip, I had stumbled from place to place asking myself what I was doing here, but that day, on the grassy hilltop, the place where those young soldiers gave their lives to avoid brutalization of their souls, I somehow feel reassured that my decision to come here made some kind of sense after all.

But the second *intifada* began eight years later, and I have not made it back. Amatallah and I wrote for a while, then she stopped when the suicide bombings began. Paul tried to explain.

"Given her politics, she probably feels some shame, and anguish, Bea."

"But, Shaheen, she should have known me better than that."

"Unfortunately, what she knew might have made her think you two stood on opposite sides of a question packed with thorns. You know how the suicide bombings are dividing so many people there and here. You could have ended up as one of the American radicals supporting them."

"That's not fair, Paul."

"You call me 'not fair', my love? I am the fairest in the land."

From one fairy tale to another we spent our nights, but during the day Paul started to steal away from me. I could feel it, and then, yes, at the start of the second *intifada*, I began to measure his leaving. Paul would never be cruel. He softened every angry word with the love I knew he had for me. Our love strong but not strong enough, for either of us. After 9/11 and the hate mail that Paul received, we made love more intensely than ever before, until we never made love again.

Paul's cousin, Moussa Hanania, lives in a modern high-rise apartment building, somewhat incongruous in its poor surroundings in Nablus. I remember Abe, my immigrant anarchist paperhanging grandfather, reminding me of how the middle classes possess the luxury of time to work out strategies. "You need that class in any struggle," he advised.

Moussa talks about humiliation, what he experiences from Israeli soldiers and how his son is frequently stopped and harassed on the street. Then he asks me about Paul.

"And, so, how is my American relative? My grandmother is very proud of him. We all hear fine things about him."

"He does good work, Professor Hanania. He is esteemed in the Palestinian community in Chicago. We hope you can visit us some time."

Hanania sighed, "My work is here."

While eating perhaps too many of the sweets than was polite, offered by his daughter, I bring up the story of the Israeli journalist who had proposed that instead of giving the $10 billion loan to Israel, Americans should give $10,000 to each homeless person in New York City. Moussa reminds me of Paul with his blunt reply.

"The homeless will get the money when they do the dirty work of the United States in the Middle East."

And then after some brief moments where professor and former students catch up, it's time for us to leave to drive back to Alena's for lunch. On the way there, I think about Paul and what role he would have taken had his grandparents not made the decision to come to America all those years ago. Would he be alive? Jailed? Practicing law? As for me, I know for certain that I'd never have been born if my grandparents hadn't had the good sense to escape Europe long before the massacres of their families in Poland. A cousin in Detroit did the research. Our relatives never made it to the Warsaw Ghetto. Instead, with other people in their town, they were lined up, shot, and buried in a mass grave.

At Alena's, the large, tasty meal of rice, spinach, meat, and pita bread overwhelms me, but I cannot refuse anything. That I know would not be polite. To eat too much is rude; to not eat enough is an insult. After some conversation, Ali reminds me about curfew, so he and I make our preparations to leave. I wish Fatima safe travel to France where she will go to visit her brother next month. Unable, as a single woman, to drink coffee in the village square, she tells me, "I will take my freedom in Paris." Although she will enjoy the cafés, I know she will return to her home and the land she loves.

Since we don't have to stop in Ramallah, Ali uses the settler's road. "Safer," he explains. With our yellow plates we are an Israeli settler couple on our way to Jerusalem for a night out. We have left America and Palestine far behind. I can be Jewish again.

Back in Jerusalem by early evening, we stop in Ali's office where photos of Martin Luther King, Jr. and Joan Baez along with posters in several languages line the wall. A complete set of Gandhi's writings occupies half of a shelf.

What do I think, Leah? Non-violent resistance. Violent resistance. No resistance. What do I think?

Jerusalem should be an international city, a place where the stillness of peace could illumine the rest of the world, where Gandhi's teachings and practices could find a home in a real institute of learning, a place where Paul's three-day weekend idea could begin an invigorated planetary partnership.

"If the Muslims, Jews, and Christians could all unite, we would celebrate Sabbath from Friday through Sunday. No labor strikes, no stones, no walls, no bombs, just a miracle."

"Like Jerusalem becoming an international city."

"And Palestine a democratic, secular state."

I love Paul because he makes of tragedy a joke, reducing the unbearable to a practical matter. He turns the sacred into the mundane, a holy war into a profane peace. Keeping to the basics allows a people to survive in the face of horror. Jewish humor. Arab humor. The humor of those who persist after anyone else would have submitted a long time ago. I miss Paul at this moment because somehow when I am with him I feel miracles can happen. But there in the shadows of Ali's office, even in the presence of historical and contemporary voices for non-violence, the elation of the day with my new friends turns to despair.

Malcolm in Yael's office; Martin on Ali's walls. The United States influences all sides of the left, as well as the right, here. I think of Yael's reminder: "Arafat is no Mandela." Despite what Randi and Michael argue about how the movements of the sixties depended too much on leaders, and despite my agreeing with them, I wish for a Mandela now, someone who could cross the waters between Malcolm and Martin with grace and the good sense to bring others along.

"A rare bird," as they used to say.

What do you think, Leah? My dearest, Leah, what do you think?

All I know is this. I had gone where I could, talked with who was willing. I had seen the determination of the Israeli government to continue building, taking over. The Israelis had deported Ali's colleague, a man committed to non-violence. Even a liberal, non-radical organization becomes a threat to the Zionist state. I can't imagine the peace talks winning anything of substance for the Palestinians.

That's where I'm afraid I end up, Leah.

Ali drops me off at a corner where I can catch a bus back to the central station and then another to Shira's sister's apartment in a small town outside Tel Aviv. We will gather there for dinner. Lunch in Palestine. Dinner in Israel. Unlike the Jerusalem-Tel Aviv express bus, this one makes numerous stops. As I settle into my seat, I pretend for a moment that I am an Israeli Jew who has spent the day working or shopping in Jerusalem. Why? I don't know. I guess I want that feeling of belonging again. This day in the West Bank has clarified and confirmed so much. More sure of my opinions about Israel's culpability, yet strangely at home here.

Yes.

At Shira's place, her sister, Lubna, feeds us small plates of different salads. After the two sisters ask me to tell them about my trip, I return to my question about the effect of so many trauma survivors, holocaust survivors, living in one place. Lubna, like Shira, agrees with my hypothesis.

"The effect is immense, Bea, and it is not just the survivors themselves, but their children. You realize that in

Israeli terms, according to what you have told me, you would be considered a child of the holocaust because all of your grandmother's family, except for the brother and sister who followed her to Chicago, perished."

"Yes, I have understood that, finally."

Lubna, a linguist at Tel Aviv University, gives me a case study of the treatment of children of survivors, which argues that when children of survivors, who have absorbed their parent's holocaust trauma, experience a later injury and begin to deal with it, the earlier indirect trauma can be healed as well. The individuation that never properly occurred can be completed. Sometimes I think all of Israel is bound to the holocaust and needs now, as it deals with its own wars, to separate from the original trauma, like so many children needing to leave behind the horrors of their parents' past.

I think about the mild clash I had with Jeffrey Eisenman's wife, Ayelet. She chided me for coming, like so many Americans, with my preconceived ideas, but I got a laugh out of her when I pointed out how only two Jews could get involved in this kind of debate. It's sport. We question, we argue, we theorize. We take pleasure in proving our case. And Americans, if they don't live in New York or Chicago, or even Los Angeles, and aren't used to us, call us loud and obnoxious, too intense. They tell us we talk too fast, too much. So we assimilate when we can, bury our oral habits and become as American as we may. In Israel I could be a Jew. In probably no other place, except New York, and, of course, Chicago could I feel so at home. But is it the land, or the community of Jews? Do we need guns for this or merely tradition, literature, associations, acceptance? A way of talking.

When I arrived at Ben Gurion airport that first evening, I stood behind an older Israeli accompanying a young Jewish man from the States. The Israeli asked the American what he thought of the airport. It was a question like Amal's—"What do you think of my country?"—plump with pride, confident the visitor will notice and admire the beauty of the host's home. The Israelis are proud of what they have done here; the Palestinians see only the stealing of their homeland. I bring to mind again Abe's old challenge about how I, too, have the privilege of living in a settler nation, and might consider atoning for it.

My grandparents spent their lives railing against the injustices of the nation state and the idea of private property. I pray that Israel will not perpetrate the genocide that made it so easy for my family to settle in America.

When I arrive back home in Chicago, I turn the dream over in my hand, the illusion, the mirage that Leah sat there listening while I traveled in what many people call the Holy Land. The heaven of their dreams twisted into a nightmare for some and a cautionary story for the rest of us.

My frame, I know, Leah, mine.

HOME

When I came home, everyone wanted to know. For years Mitch had been talking a two-state solution, and before the trip, I'd started to move in that direction. It seemed like the dream of one land and more than one people looked harder than ever. But I returned to it. I knew that to people like Ayelet Eisenman I looked like one more American Jew telling Israelis what to do. But I also saw that some Israeli Jews thought as I did. Born there. Grew up there. Not planning to leave there. They yearned for a democratic state. And they believed the one they lived in did not come close. They did not hate themselves as Jews. They did not form their opinions from the arm of a plush or bare boned chair in the corner of a writing room, or a reading room, or a classroom. And, of course, some Israeli Jews, the majority of those I met and heard about, thought this all heresy.

So, my chicanita, *my bubelah, reunited at last. And now you can love yourself while at the same time hate the hell brought to the Palestinian people by the Jewish people, they themselves tortured by recent history, and afraid. Welcome home, my Beastie. We missed you.*

What a relief to hear Danny again. Something comes alive in me when he's around.

I trust you will not mind my bringing up the fact that life presents a touchy topic for me, sweetie. And, furthermore, mija, *you are not yet free if it is still a dead man who enlivens you.*

And so I had come home to Randi's broken heart, the boyfriend who couldn't make the commitment, and then to Michael's curfew violation with the Chicago police. When he started to complain, I wanted to blurt out how he had no idea what a curfew violation in Nablus could mean. But I caught myself, realizing that he knew enough to know the difference between the effects of this minor infraction on his life and the possible fatal outcomes of such an action on a young black kid on the West Side, or down our own block. I had come home—well not literally—to Mitch who I think seemed the most relieved that I was back. And I came home to Paul, at least for a while. No one seemed to notice any difference in me except for the ethereals.

You are not so guilty, not so anxious, Beatrice.

Emma got why Danny pushed me to go to Israel. Of course, he had to use the ploy that I would carry back with me first hand stories of deprivation and worse. But Danny—the medic of salty wounds, the comic of earthly affairs—knew what I didn't know would happen. "Take the stones out of your heart and what you are, you will be, and will love." *Who* said that?

You, *my bubelah.*

Sadly, nothing changed with Leah. Perhaps it even worsened. Though I promised myself I'd keep from arguing about Israel at Passover that year, I saw the space between us widen. Less politics and fewer arguments, which meant not much humor to relieve the arguments. We kept conversation controlled, careful. Leah talked about Raoul's Bar Mitzvah the next winter.

"You'll come, won't you, Bicie?"

"Of course, I wouldn't miss it."

"It's just that I know you and Mitch don't observe, and I know what you think."

With someone else this might constitute bait, but Leah was too honest for that.

"Leah, with Dad gone, someone has to sit in the congregation and *kibitz* everyone about Mr. and Mrs. Hutzy Klutz."

Leah laughed. It was good to hear her laugh her inimitable laugh. I didn't realize how much I had missed it as our détente developed. Anyway, I knew that Howard's style of gentle teasing, so free of malice, wouldn't hurt her, and she knew I'd go no further than that. To us "Hutzy Klutz" stood for "Hypo Crit." No one would deny there weren't a few of those in every congregation, no matter the denomination, religion, sect, creed, and so forth.

I had always wanted Paul to join us at Passover. Mitch would have been okay with it. After all, any time he was dating someone Jewish, she'd come along. His gentile girlfriends didn't last, too much homey in my ex-husband. But Paul resisted.

"Bea, you have enough to worry about with Leah. You don't need your Palestinian lover and former professor to complicate the meal."

Andrea and Cheryl never understood my relationship with Paul, though they accepted it, with the grace they showed me from the day I quit the make-up lessons all those years ago. Andrea, in a greatly improved second marriage and Cheryl, married now to an ad exec in the agency she worked for, thought I should rejoin the club. Either in a second attempt with Mitch, or something legal and more traditional with Paul. They believed in loyalty and commitment. After all, despite my obsession with Israel and Palestine, my odd romantic relationships, my inability to make small talk anywhere, they would never leave me. Friendship, family, that's what makes a life worthwhile, they would argue. And I loved them for that. They could not comprehend how I lived only with my children, had regular sex with my companion, colleague, lover, on the other side of town, and occasional sex with my ex-husband, who lived around the block.

"Bicie, why don't you just choose one or the other. Either one is perfectly fine for us. Move Paul in or go back to Mitch. Of course, Mitch is our preference for obvious reasons, but Paul is a good man. Just choose, Bicie. This half way here and half way there is not good for your mental health," Andrea admonished me with Cheryl nodding emphatically.

My friends Gwen and Nita got it a lot easier.

The universe must have programmed me for two friends at a time, making me a member of an intense triumvirate, twice. Gwen and Nita, the friends I met the year Mom died, have somehow taken the place that Andrea and Cheryl occupied in those growing up years. A and C will never leave my side, but the two of them have to bend their "nice Jewish girls who grew up in Chicago" boundaries to include me. They try not to ask too many questions, though we did have one serious long talk about multiple lovers and AIDS and if I knew that I was sleeping with everyone Mitch and Paul were sleeping with. I had to explain that Paul didn't bring anyone else home, that Mitch stayed celibate after our divorce for several years.

By the time he started to date again, his dating practices included the benefits of testing and condoms, his usual good instincts and a taste for caution.

As you know, dearest Beast, in the state in which I reside, regrets do not weigh on me. I am pleased that those practices saved many, that now medication at least treats surviving friends and others quite well. But I will say, so you don't have to, that the disease which closed down my hand, though it can find its way into anyone's bloodstream, destroys in unequal proportions.

So, as Danny alluded, the AIDS conversation took a different turn in the gay community and in Chicago's black community, where Gwen and Nita grew up.

During my sophomore year in college, I moved back home to be closer with Mom after she got the terminal diagnosis, to help Dad with Leah, and to deal with the desperate understanding that my mother, on whom I had depended like no one else, was going to leave me.

Gwen, Nita, and I met in a U.S. History course at the Chicago campus of the University of Illinois. Solid fans of the charismatic professor's lectures, we all struck up a conversation after class one day. Nita and I were history majors, thinking then about teaching, and he inspired us. Gwen and Nita knew a good preacher when they heard one. Dr. Arthur invited the three of us to his church in South Shore so we could hear one of his actual sermons. Though I had followed Howard's way and rejected organized religion, when Mom was dying, prayer seemed like a good idea. Baptist, Jewish, Buddhist. Whatever. It didn't work. She died. But I saw the comfort that religion offered people, and I learned closer up how the African American church served as a site for political organizing.

Nita took one of those winding paths from history major to filmmaker. Luckily, she landed a solid faculty position teaching broadcast journalism at Chicago State. She married the boy next door, divorced him, and then married him again. They moved to the suburbs when their son started to get in some trouble.

One day after looking at the footage Nita had gathered to do a documentary on Harold Washington, the city's first black mayor, her son Johnny became inspired. When he finishes law school, he plans on entering the civic life, a cleaned up way to say he will get his bruises in the city where the old machine, once defeated, has resurrected and refashioned itself. A dynasty we fought so hard, in those heady days of campaigning for Harold Washington.

Working on the campaign with Nita helped me put myself back together that year with Danny gone, Howard gone, and my marriage done. Washington succeeded in knocking out the bloody machine ward warriors and then dropped dead, barely into his second term, just as he began to extend the small gains he had struggled to make. We all mourned. People say that, in addition to getting his name on the new main library, a college, and a park, his real legacy is Barack Obama. A pragmatist, like Washington, Obama...

Anachronism alert, anachronism alert.

Danny, sometimes time just seeps through history, blurring those artificial boundaries, okay? Back to 1992, coming home, and reminiscing about the past. For God's sake, Danny, where am I now, *actually*? I think in the 70s, so I will continue there for a moment.

Gwen married a white guy she met at Dr. Arthur's church and moved to Gary. Her Methodist minister father railed at the white and the Baptist but settled down when she gave him three grandsons in five years. She and her husband Dave run an urban ministry where she says the homeless women, many of them former prostitutes, have taught her the humility she preaches back to anyone who will listen. Always an observer who could tell you where you were going before you knew it, she listens in a way that makes me carefully pick out my words in her presence.

And I want you to know that I have always approved of your girlsomes. You might try mixing them more, you know.

It didn't work, Danny. You know I tried.

Andrea and Cheryl just couldn't make the cross over, even Andrea, my pro-integration debate partner in the eighth grade. Racism, in its subtle and not so subtle doses, wins again. Andrea and Cheryl's families ran from the South Side to Skokie when blacks started moving in. Howard stayed and watched the value of our home fall due to the manipulations of realtors aided by the racism of people like the parents of my friends.

Now Chicago has started to experience an insidious reversal. Throughout my conscious childhood Richard J. Daley had been mayor. He was mayor when I entered the third grade. He was mayor when Mitch and I got banged around in Lincoln Park in 1968, and he was mayor until a week and a half before Randi and Michael were born. With Daley's son, Richard M. or Richard II, getting elected in 1989, we felt the worst kind of *déjà vu*, the kind that feels more like lucid nightmare than some frayed firing of the brain. His reign may top the record of his father's twenty-one years. Outwardly Chicago has changed a lot. Like other cities that got "revitalized," Chicago didn't go the way of Detroit, but the way it went meant that condos replaced public housing, poor blacks had fewer places to live, and flowers bloomed on Michigan Avenue.

We know, Beastie. You love the garden and hate the gardener. And to return to your return from Israel and Palestine, and all that.

Yes, Danny. So those eight years, between my return and the second *intifada,* saw Randi and Michael graduate high school and college and Mitch and me comfort one another as we united to watch over a depression Randi encountered at twenty that surprised us all and track the peaking of Michael's anger that year and then its waning two years later. At first, my relationship with Paul deepened after I returned from Israel and Palestine. He loved that I had seen the land of his origins, if not his birth. He saw the shift in me that Danny had been angling for, not so self-punishing. I started to join him in working on some of his Middle East immigration cases.

But then things began slowly to change between us.

Eight years after my travels, in September 2000, Ariel Sharon** made his own trip to the Temple Mount, site of the Dome of the Rock and al-Aqsa Mosque. Palestinians all saw it as provocation. Probably the most contested sacred space, the Mount represented Sharon's attempt to show right-wing Jews that they could count on him. A month later on a Saturday morning, Paul sat down across from me at his kitchen table where I had poured myself a bowl of cereal.

---

* A special Israeli investigative commission held Sharon responsible for allowing the Phalangist massacre at the Sabra and Shatila refugee camps in southern Lebanon in 1982, which caused him to lose his job as defense minister, but months after his action at Temple Mount, in 2001, he was elected prime minister.

"Laila and Ahmed are moving to Ramallah."

"What?"

"Well, it shouldn't come as such a surprise. You know Ahmed feels a responsibility to help his parents. They are aging. He is the oldest son. This Sharon thing has agitated them. He proposed a plan where Laila and Nisreen would live with him there in the summer, but Laila would not even consider it."

"I understand, but how will this affect Nisreen?"

"She will learn to know her people, the land she comes from, why her father closes himself in a closet a few times a year so he can sob himself to sleep. And he's been offered a position in a kind of Palestinian think tank. They do research, some publishing, some activism. It gives him a perch so that he can return."

I touched Paul's hand, but he drew it away. I had never experienced that kind of coldness from him before.

"Bea, I'm sorry. I just can't stand that they will be so far from here. I worry about the danger they will face."

"I know, Shaheen."

And then he took my hand and kissed it and began to cry.

"Bea, it pains my heart so that Rashida never saw Laila grow into a woman, never knew Nisreen. And now I am losing them, too."

He pulled away for a second time as he brought himself back to his usual equanimity.

"I am sorry, Bea. I love you more than I thought possible when we first took up so improbably and so cautiously, but these things which I have tried to bear, and manage, yes, manage, break through from time to time, you know."

"Of course, Shaheen, I know. Together we will concentrate on Laila and Ahmed and Nisreen. We'll help them pack. We'll gather all the friends and relatives. We'll make sure they know they have everyone's blessings."

So, my dear Beatrice, you see about this pull for people in exile. Whether forced or chosen, return always lurches in front of them as possibility. It never leaves the mind. The old place has its way with many of us. You think I didn't have my own heart surge when I faced the European continent after all those years away?

In her gentle way Emma meant to warn me about the future's brute news. My love would leave me for the exile of return. Born in Bridgeview, Illinois, Paul Shaheen charted his origins on a dream map, somewhere in Jerusalem, not far from where Sharon stomped around the Temple Mount. In a neighborhood where generations of his family had crossed from one side of the street to the other, greeting their Arab, Jewish, and Christian friends.

His announcement came officially a few months after the Trade Center attacks, but I always marked the end of our time together as that conversation when he told me his daughter would leave Chicago for Palestine. Paul had reached retirement age. He believed his daughter and granddaughter needed him. He knew he needed them. He had measured our time together from the start.

"We have been good for each other, Bea. And now we will make our returns. I to Palestine and you to Mitch."

"You're acquainting a homeland with an ex-husband?"

And then I got it. Mitch wasn't Palestine's equivalent. Rashida was. In the end, after all the just causes and lost causes and sacrifices and speeches, personal and public, in the end, our beloveds, our children, and parents, and grandparents are what we live for. Sometimes people cross over for good making the bridge the dwelling place for all that love, but some people cross back. Sojourners. It takes all kinds.

You don't always know the last time you will make love to somebody. Sometimes you don't get that you're in the middle of a one-night stand with someone you had—earlier in the evening–sized up to be the love, or at least *a* love, of your life, or you don't realize that you're about to be dumped, or you didn't figure out that this romantic involvement you are currently involved in is actually and thoroughly played out. Sometimes the other person knows; sometimes the last stand surprises your soon to be ex-lover as much as it does you. But when you really know, and you *both* really know that this is the last time you will make love, after a long and complicated and thrilling and difficult relationship, it's like you actually *are* the last two lovers on this puny earth and the explosion between you will launch a new one.

My dear, I have wanted you to be less chaste all along in this story, but perhaps your use of common hyperbole doesn't quite fit. I mean, after all, you and Paul by then were mature adults.

Emma, you're going to have to give me this, okay? This is real. What Paul and I had together meant something to each of us that neither of us could talk about, so maybe that last time, that last night gave us the space to give each other what long conversations–about our children who lived completely different lives and then developed an affection for each other, and our daily law practices that started nations away from each other and then traveled along the same patterned path—could never do. So indulge me, please, my dear ghosts and guides.

My tangled heart and uncertain legs wrap themselves around your half-healed fear. Your mouth pushes up against me, brushing away the only time I ever cried in your presence. A vision sweeps over us and considers planting a new religion but instead leaves it to rot in a pagan forest where new growth emerges despite what anyone could have predicted.

Bubelah, *you have grown. At last,* mija, mi chicanita, *my Beastie, Leah's Bicie, Emma's Beatrice, Shaheen's…*

Enough, Danny!

So I took on some of Paul's practice, hired one of our old law school's fresh graduates who spoke Arabic, expanded the little Monadnock suite into three small offices and a waiting room, watched my children become adults, prayed for a reconciliation with my sister, and thought about dating Mitch.

At dinner one night, Nita nodded approval. Gwen simply said, "Time." And Andrea and Cheryl, when I called them? Just guess. They *kvelled.*

And for the non-Yiddish speakers, bubelah?

They were as happy and proud as if I were their eldest child getting married.

But lurking still, like my heart seized and shaking on a dark night away from home, my sister's sorrow and what some might call her madness.

JOURNALS: 3

As soon as I heard Eli's voice, I knew things had shifted again.

"Bicie, at first it seemed like the teaching had brought the old Leah back, but when the semester ended, she disappeared again. And now the journals are closer to home. They frighten me. She talks about drugs and guns, here, or close to here, on the border. The murders of the women in Mexico.** Ciudad Juárez. You've heard about them?"

"Yes, Eli. I had one client who was desperate to find out about his young cousin. I got word to an attorney friend in Texas, but we didn't have any luck."

"It is a tragedy. I didn't know, but now I do because of Leah's watch. And from Mexico, Bicie, she has now come home to Los Angeles. She pastes newspaper articles about the murders in South Central into her journals and then, Bicie, she describes the prisons to which the convicted ones go as 'concentration camps'."

"Concentration camps?"

"Yes. One time she wrote about a young man sent to juvenile hall for nothing, maybe a small amount of marijuana. There he was raped. He came out, bought a gun, joined a gang, killed someone and got sent to prison for

---

** Since the early 90s, nearly 500 young women, many of them indigenous, women who had come from rural areas to the city across the border from El Paso to work in the maquiladoras—the border factories bred by NAFTA—had been raped and murdered, sometimes disappeared.

life. Not innocent, not like the Jews, but like the Jews, she'd say. Can you believe that, Bicie? A gang member like the Jews?"

"Yes, Eli, I believe it."

A long silence came between us.

"Bicie, there were others. Complete innocence. Drugs planted on them by police. Sentenced to long years in jail. That injustice, I understand. Like the Jews, but the murderers, Bicie?"

"Each one of those murderers, Eli, is responsible, but so are we. How they got to that point. That's what she's meaning, Eli. But how did she make this jump from international holocausts? I mean it's something I would do. But Leah?"

"Bicie, she writes about the young men she sees on the streets on her way home from the flea market who could be dead that night. And then one morning we had this conversation. It was the first time she brought into our everyday life the subject matter of the journals."

I marveled at the patience of my brother-in-law. Anyone else who had a wife going through what Leah was going through would have filled her up with medication, locked her up, left her, or all of the afore-named alternatives, but not Leah's Eli. What perfect luck and love my dear little sister had. I wanted to weep.

"She started to press me, Bicie. One after another question. 'What made a Nazi, Eli? When did fear become socio-pathology? What Paul called war, remember, Eli? What could be done? At which age and how could a person intervene?' She asked herself, and then me, these questions so many times, I became ill with her burden,

Bicie. I could only respond that I believed evil was real, that it stalked a few and when the rest of us fell asleep or became too afraid, it stalked more of us. That would satisfy her, but then the next day she'd be back. The good thing, though, she was talking."

I thought about Eli living alone with the journals, and these mostly one-sided conversations, interrogations.

"You know, last year, Bicie, when you told her about the conference at the University of Chicago Law School on police brutality that Michael was working on, she didn't say much to you."

"Right. It surprised me, Eli. Usually, at least, she would have commented on the injustice. She never lost her sense for that even if she could not act. Or her interest in any of the children and their projects."

"Well, Bicie, she created an entire journal about every scrap she could find on line about the proceedings. Her words? 'The Nazis have come back. Perhaps they have never left. We're only safe because someone else suffers at the top of the list. Young black men and women, Mexicans, Native Americans. How far up on the list are the Jews? Not even as close as the gypsies were on our list. Are we down by the righteous Christians who spoke up and risked their lives in Europe on our behalf? Jews are still on the list, Eli, farther up if we speak up. At least my Bicie and her son are doing that. And what have I done? What am I doing? Nothing. Nothing. Nothing. And even if we don't speak up, we're on that list.' And then at the bottom, Bicie, there was a small note: '9/11 Muslims'."

So when Leah and Eli arrived at the house, I kept hearing the words that Eli had read to me over the phone. He had copied them out of her journal, the first time he had done that. I knew things were serious for him to make this further trespass. But I promised myself that I would remain calm and welcoming.

"Good *Yontif*, Bicie."

Eli spoke. Leah looked sad, distracted. Thoreau's "we all lead lives of quiet desperation," or something like that, pushed through my brain. But we go on. Is this what he meant? Or is this worse? Anyway, we went on, hugs, holiday greetings.

"So how is Oberlin treating you, Raoul?"

"Actually, not half bad, Aunt Bicie."

Raoul, always a little shy, but polite, sweet, had started to look more and more like Howard, and he was even developing our dad's ability to put other people at ease with a few words. Not the words themselves but how he said them. I wonder if my dad had been shy before he met Rosie. Mom always said she pulled him out of his shell. Maybe that's what she meant. My mind wandered to my own son.

I had come to pick Michael up from his dorm freshman year to go home for the summer. He was all packed up and went into the hall to say good-bye to some friends. So I looked around the dorm room, bereft of posters and bedding and computers and the other tangled mess of young men innocent, lucky, not at war, leaving the luxury of college for the luxury of home and a summer job, and then I saw it on the bulletin board above Michael's desk, the photograph of a lovely young woman. Everything else removed, just that photo hanging there. His way of telling me he had someone. I always had to read between his lines and the signs, like this picture. He wanted me to ask. So I did. And he told me. He told me her name, but that was all. That was enough for now. My own shy son.

"So, Bicie, we're just stopping here to say hello, and then we're off to our temporary little home in Hyde Park. The wonders of the internet and a resourceful niece. Thanks to Randi, Leah will even have an entire kitchen to herself."

"Well, I'm always happy to grant her complete charge over mine, but I know it's more fun for her to roam alone and not have to deal with my nerves."

Instead of staying with me as they usually did, they had gotten for themselves, or Randi had gotten for them, a little apartment, a month-long sublet in a building a block away from us. Eli and Raoul would stay the customary week, but Leah, ominous, will spend the month. Their building, called "The Tuileries," reminded me of how Mom used to joke about Marie Antoinette's gardens when she planted the flowers in our back yard. Lakeshore Drive became the French Riviera, and our yard, a royal garden. My mother could transport you anywhere from here. How we all missed that.

Then I came back from there to here as Eli asked me, in a whisper, to meet him on 53rd Street at a coffee shop after they dropped off their bags. What he said out loud, more innocuous.

"Leah will unpack and set up the apartment, Raoul will make our electronic connections with his laptop, and I will walk the streets of Hyde Park where there is not a palm tree in sight."

Later when I turned the corner onto 53rd Street, I saw Eli waiting outside. Once settled in a booth at the coffee spot, he dropped his earlier breeziness in favor of his actual fears and feelings. He had been waiting to talk to me for a while.

"Bicie, I'm afraid the journals are no longer enough. Leah has become despondent. Since Passover lands on Ida's *yahrzeit*, she says she wants to spend some time with you, go to the cemetery and the conservatory in Garfield Park. She seems to be stuck in the ancient past of Rosie and Howard's West Side childhood. I don't know. Something doesn't feel right."

"What are you saying, Eli?"

"I don't know for sure. I just need you to understand how fragile she has become. At first the journals kept her safe, if not completely sane, but now I think they have approached the law of diminishing returns. She appears consumed with guilt. Please go easy on her."

"Don't worry, Eli. Your sister-in-law has matured."

"I didn't mean to offend you, Bicie."

"No offense taken, Eli. I just wanted to reassure you,"

"You know this whole 60 years of Israel celebrations everywhere you look and then the Palestinians calling it the Nakba, the catastrophe. She doesn't know what to do with all of this. She still believes in the Jewish state. But her journal travels have taken her to a place where she does not appear able to make a reconciliation."

"Perhaps, together, she and I can do that."

"Bicie, I plead with you again. Be careful."

"My dearest, Eli, I hope you know that, no matter our disagreements, my sister and I together occupy a realm like no other. No one shares this space with me. Not my beloved children. Not Mitch. Not Paul. Not my friends who sustain me. Not my causes that equip me. It is the ancient land of Rosie and Howard, and their love. Only Leah knows that love, that home, those years. I would do nothing to hurt her. I could not trample that sacred space."

"Well, Bicie, that gives me comfort, but please pay attention. I don't want to say what I am worried about. I don't want to think what could happen."

"Are you talking suicide, Eli?"

"So you see how serious I think it has become."

"I see, Eli. I will pay attention."

Eli returned to their apartment, and I made my way back home when I realized that I had started to shake. I had given my word to Eli, but I wasn't sure what that meant. This time I called no one. I told no one. I hinted at nothing. I knew I had to remain alone with all of this. And, with the disappearance of Danny and Emma, I felt more on my own than ever. I could not conjure a joke, a complaint, a mild attack from either of them. No words from that beyond, just my own mind, which needed quieting more than I thought I might have the capacity for. So, instead, I went home to read out of Leah's journal. Eli had gone from spying to trespassing to blatant theft. And why I thought this would quiet me, I do not know. But, you know what? It brought me to a steely peace. Oxymoron? No. Just wait. And so I read to you, dear reader, what my sister wrote.

Where can I find a place to trust these fears? I used to close my head to Bicie's rants, and now I discover ones of my own construction. What happened to our people? When did ordinary evil become extraordinary? When did simple-minded ignorance and intolerance, combined

with a long-suffering history, turn into a machine, a system? A shadowy double of the hatred that ran the camps? The will and wish to end my people, who give me the will and wish to carry on despite what sought to destroy them. I dig a hole, one circle inlaid inside another to bury myself in. Bicie always said if someone hates Arabs, they hate Jews, and if someone hates Jews, they hate Arabs. And what does it mean when Jews hate Arabs and Arabs hate Jews? We live inside a candle that has melted half way, and we know we die when it collapses, yet we let it burn and watch with sickened pleasure and confused delight the shapes the wax takes all around us. How can we not see ourselves twisting, distorted by the flame our fear keeps lit? And most of us wish no harm. Only a few possess the capabilities to sustain such bitterness. But if we don't stop them, where do we end up? Melted into a heap, or moaning at its edges? Running from it, or making apologies and promises that we didn't know and would never do it again anyway? I know some young Germans who have tired from their parents' guilt and others who have decided they will help Palestinians to show they know how to do the right thing this time. But deep inside I worry that the legacy of Jew hatred has not disappeared, and now they have a cover for it. And so many others who fight for Bicie's noble cause. Are some of them, many of them, Jew haters? And my sister herself and her self-righteous friends? That Deborah, for example. How did I get to this place? I always knew the uncertainty would gain in the end. I knew where this writing would go. Back to where it began.

The holocaust. Whose holocaust? "All of them, my sweet. But some are worse than others, my love." And the cynics who claim Jews put money to end the geno-cide in Darfur only to remind the world that the Israelis aren't so bad, to remind the world that Muslims know how to massacre. Who had to be reminded? But what have we become? Like Tippie Hedrin in "The Birds." When they pulled her out of the attic where she almost got pecked to death, she fought the ones who brought her out. Traumatized, she couldn't distinguish the one who would kill her from the one who would save her. But what if the ones who save you created the conditions they rescue you from. What if the birds are innocent? What if evil is innocent? What if the guilty are the good ones who name the evil and try to escape it? What if the only way to manage evil is to let it roll over you and get up when it has passed? What if we were right when we knew "This too shall pass" and wrong when we cried "Never again"? But we cannot bend our heads and go through the doors of our own damnation. How do we struggle and not become the ones we struggle against?

Perhaps the Palestinians are the Germans who are the Jews who are the Palestinians and the seventh circle embraces them all. Perhaps we all remain stuck there, and all else just an illusion of perfection. The rose, the blessed flower. Where roses grow wild, we think we can rest. May I rest my head with my mother, and may my sister understand my struggle and why I had to leave this earth. I thought this writing would keep me alive. The recording of all the horrors. The way to face them and face myself. But I returned to my own self-hatred. The demon. The devil. The Jew. I am the Jew and I am dirty. I am the darkness and I have sinned. Forgive my darkness. Forgive my sin. And turn this earth back into the ball of fire so it can burn itself out, purifying itself like the dark that has no enemy, only itself. Like the dark that sees without any lamp or light or goodly, godly flame. I cannot get out of this, cannot shake it, and can no longer pretend that I can.

This is where it stopped. I knew I had to find her. I called her cell, but Raoul answered. He was almost hysterical.

"Aunt Bicie, my mother left a note."

"What are you saying Raoul? Where is your father?"

I could hear myself screaming. People were looking at me on the steps of the library, where I'd gone to read the journals, the place I used to take Randi and Michael when they were little, for storytelling hour. The place where they went, when they got older but not old enough to be home alone, to do their homework.

"He hasn't come back yet. I thought you were going to meet him."

"I did, but he said something about going downtown, that your mother had asked him to search for a book for her at that place she likes near Orchestra Hall."

"Yeah, I was supposed to go with him, but we missed signals or something. You know my dad, not the best at plans. I'd said something about going to the museum. It got confused. I just went down to the store to get some food. I think my mother thought I'd gone with him. Aunt Bicie, I was just getting ready to call you. I didn't want to open this note alone."

"Well, don't Raoul. I'm only a few blocks away at the library. I'll be there in a minute. Call your dad."

"That's the problem, Bicie. He left his cell phone here."

"Then call the bookstore and leave him a message to get back here."

"I did that already. They said he had already left."

"Well, at least, he's on his way."

I hoped more than anything I would not have to search for her. I wrote down all the places she might be. The cemetery. The museums. The conservatory in Garfield Park. The Monadnock. I shivered to think she might consider trying to find a way to throw herself down the stairway shaft there. But I'd start at the little apartment they'd rented. The Tuileries. *The royal gardens, Mom. I will start there and then circle back around.* By the time I got there, Raoul had opened the envelope. His face drained, and his eyes moving back and forth across the room as if he might find a trace of his mother in this rented place.

"She says how much she loves us, that she didn't want to hurt us, but that she was trying so hard for so long…"

I put my arms around him, hoping that we still had time. Eighteen years old, and a young eighteen, Raoul should probably not be doing this with me. I called Mitch who, thankfully, was at home and asked him to come and get Raoul. He arrived, pale, panicked.

"What can I do, Bicie?"

I took him into the hall.

"Right now, I want you to be with Raoul. Take him home. Eli is on his way back here. He can help me figure out what to do. I'm going to start with this building."

"Okay, Bicie. But call me as soon as Eli gets here. Let me know what's happening."

"I will, Mitch."

We came back into the apartment where Raoul had started to pace.

"I should have known. We should have known…"

Mitch went over to him and put his arms around him.

"This is not your fault, not anyone's fault."

"That's what she said in the note."

I hugged Raoul as hard as I could, trying to reassure him.

"Raoul, I'm going to find her, and I'm going to find her alive."

As he and Mitch left, I refused to let myself face what this would all mean if I failed him, if I failed all of us. So, instead, I thought as calmly and as carefully as I could. I knew that a note meant it was serious. She had a plan, and she was intending to act on it. But the note gave no clue about what she intended to do. I started walking around the apartment, thinking that I might find something that could help me, knowing that I should also be calling the police but figuring that waiting for them and then talking to them would waste time, which we had little of. I found myself getting hot, so I opened a window. And then I heard it. Chopin. On the fire escape. A good choice, I thought, as I climbed out the window.

For an instant I saw Leah's body floating down as if from the roof, then, at the far edge of my vision, in the left eye, a small flash of light. *I'm too late. She's gone.* But then I heard her humming.

And there she was, with her feet on an iron stair, sitting on the roof of a building named for a royal garden, in the neighborhood that had sheltered all the people lying in that cemetery, the one Leah chose not to run to, not yet, at least. My beloved baby sister had hesitated. She had not jumped. As I made it out the window as quietly as I could, I saw her yellow skirt and her hair blowing and her arm holding on to the railing, and I began to cry, softly, as softly as I could. She looked like she did in college, pulling one hand down now to try to gather her skirt in the wind, with a cigarette in the other and the Chopin tape playing on the bottom step. I moved slowly and steadily around the tape player and up the fire escape, not wanting to alarm her but needing to get close enough so she would have to look me in the eye. When she finally saw me, she reached out to me, and then I knew it was all right.

"Bicie, you came to save me. But a miracle happened. I stood up to jump, and then I couldn't do it. I couldn't leave Eli. I thought Raoul might be better off. He could go on. He would have many good memories and would not have me as a burden as he tried to make a life for himself. His crazy, depressed mother. He would be ashamed of me in front of his girlfriends. Better off without my up the stairs, down the basement *mishegoss*. In time, he would heal, like you did with Mom. He's old enough, now."

I touched her hand, but she brushed it away.

"But Eli, Bicie, how could I leave him? In the eighth grade he let me read *A Tale of Two Cities* aloud to him on the bus going home from the downtown library. He followed me to Ann Arbor and then to Los Angeles. He would not let me go. I do not know why...Bicie...how do you live here with all the ghosts? How do you do it?"

She should *only* know. And where *are* they? Why won't they help me now?

On your own, Beastie.

183

A whisper. Then Danny disappeared again, and I was alone again with Leah.

"Bicie, I do not know what happened up there, but, yes, a miracle, I believe. I stood up thinking about Eli and Raoul, and the rest of you, Bicie, and then I heard these voices, two voices.

"Voices, Leah?"

"Yes. Two boys, maybe twelve and fourteen, were dragging this old, moldy mattress to the dumpster down below. They were complaining about their mother."

"Let's just leave it here."

"Naw, we can't do that."

"Sure, they'll pick it up from here. Mom'll never know. We got it close enough. No way I'm gonna lift this thing and get its cooties all over me. Just drop it right here."

"Here?"

"Yea. Here."

"Look, Bicie. They made a bed for me below. I floated down and lay in it and rested. I lay down in it and lived. Then you came out the window, and I saw I had never left."

I was quiet, saying nothing, because I knew she had much more to tell me. There was silence between us for a while. Leah lit her cigarette. Chopin kept playing, or someone playing Chopin kept playing.

So, finally, Bicie, my beloved sister, my mentor, my torturer, you let me speak. All this time and no one hardly heard my voice. Everything through your eyes. Eli talks, even Mitch, Paul, your friends, and all this time, this entire story, and barely two words from me. Bicie, this is not fair. Well, I say, let Leah speak.

And so she did. All afternoon, after she let me call Mitch who met Eli on the street before he could come up to the apartment and interrupt us.

"Mitch, I've got to go up. She needs me."

"She's safe, Eli. The Rubenstein girls have each other. I learned a long time ago not to interfere."

"What are you talking about, Mitch? Bicie is strong, but look at what Leah was about to do."

"And she didn't."

"Raoul, Bicie, they saved her."

"No one saves anyone else. It's taken me years to understand that, my friend. Years."

THE RUBENSTEIN GIRLS ESCAPE THE FIRE BY TALKING THEIR WAY THROUGH THE FLAMES

So my beloved Leah spoke, and I listened.

"Bicie, last semester I taught a graduate seminar at USC."

"I know."

"On Emily Dickinson."

"I know."

"So you and Eli talk?"

"We talk."

"I had this student, Bicie. Even Eli doesn't know about her."

"Yes?"

"She reminded me of myself in graduate school. Agitated and captivated. Half the time I could not take my mind out of the poems I was plowing through, and the other half I could not sustain the concentration each poem demanded. I paced. I second-guessed myself. I made Eli miserable. And then I'd dive back in and swim for hours, gleeful, until the next round of punishment, self-inflicted torture. I traveled from pure pleasure to utter agony, sometimes more than once a day. It's curious, almost, that I ever finished. And then I collapsed. Pulled out. Retreated. I thought it was the only way I could survive.

But this girl, this young woman–her name is Meena–has shown me there is another. Or at least for her...I don't know. Bicie, for a while I thought I understood something, but I seemed to have lost it. It was my last hope. I was hanging on for many years, digging further and further into wars, genocides, holocausts. I could not quit. And I did nothing, nothing for anyone. I was a good mother, and mostly a good wife, and sometimes a good friend, and hardly ever a good sister."

I tried to say something, but Leah was vigilant.

"But I did nothing about all of these horrors that I could not quit researching and documenting. I was obsessed, Bicie. I assume you know about the journals. When I realized that Eli had been reading them, I thought I would disintegrate right then. So you know about them, yes?"

"Yes, Leah, I know about them."

"How much?

"Not much more than you just told me," I lied.

"So this seminar, it was a wonder for me, brought me to life again. To prepare I had to dig back to all the work on Dickinson since I quit. Back to the mines, but the light was good. I stayed unexpectedly focused as I read everything I could find last summer. There's all this work about Dickinson and the war, Dickinson and abolition, even Dickinson and the holocaust. Paul Celan–you remember when I read you aloud his poems?"

"Of course, Leah. We were facing the Pacific and this blue light sort of enveloped you as you read."

"You weren't on anything, Bicie?"

"Swear to God."

At least we could still joke.

"Well…Celan translated Dickinson into German, which I had known, of course, but I didn't know that people had started to read her almost as a holocaust poet. She haunted Celan the way she haunted me, and people were looking at her understanding of trauma more closely. So I put together a lecture on the criticism that examines their affinities, Celan and Dickinson, and then Meena, the young woman in my seminar I mentioned, asked me if she could write her seminar paper on Mahmoud Darwish and Dickinson."

Leah stopped to take a moment with her cigarette.

"Do you know him, Professor?

"Yes, yes, I do, Meena,"

"So can I talk with you about my plan?

"Certainly, Meena."

"Thankful that your Paul had introduced me to Darwish, I asked her if we could make an appointment in my office and to send me an e-mail briefly outlining her idea. I needed time to think. Of course, I knew I could not deny her. She was one of the smartest kids in the seminar. But could I handle it? That's what I didn't know. I will not go into the details of her victorious analysis right now. As much as I tried to convert you to poetry, I don't think I succeeded."

"You'd be surprised."

"Well, you'd be surprised about where this young woman brought me."

"Where?"

"Mentally and politically, to a place you could identify with. Physically, to a demonstration."

"What kind of demonstration?"

"I mentioned she was Palestinian, yes?"

"No."

"Well, she was. She is."

"So we stayed in touch after the semester ended. I came around, Bicie. I was converted."

Leah stopped talking and stared out from that fire escape to the lake and over to our dad's old building–the one he moved to after Mom died–and to the trees in Jackson Park.

"Converted, Leah?"

"I went with Meena to a demonstration protesting the blockade of Gaza. Bicie, medical supplies, food. Life support machines. Dialysis patients."

"I know, Leah."

Then she became almost wistful.

"At the demonstration Meena and some others decided they were going to do civil disobedience, to get arrested. For some reason the police took a long time to come around. Meena and a couple of her friends got tired, so they lay down on the street with their arms linked. Bicie, it reminded me of a slumber party, the three of them chattering away. I thought of you and Andrea and Cheryl, when you were in high school. They'd spend the night, and you would all talk past midnight. I never knew how long because I'd finally fall asleep. I hoped I could be like all of you someday, thinking it nearly impossible that I would be that grown up. These young women on the asphalt, Bicie, like at a slumber party. They are children, Bicie."

Then she started sobbing.

"But I don't know what to do. These are our people in danger and our people doing these awful things. Medical supplies, food. Why would they do it? So I thought I would come here this year and talk to you about my conversion, but instead I became very depressed, Bicie. Like what I was holding in all these years finally blew apart. I had no direction. No home. No purpose."

By then, the Chopin tape had clicked off, and all we could hear was an occasional car pulling away from the four way stop below. After a few minutes of that quiet, Leah started talking again.

"Bicie, do you remember how Ida used to save silver dollars for us? Every time she got one from a customer, she'd pocket it and replace it with a paper bill when she turned in her receipts at the end of the day."

I nodded, knowing what was coming.

"So you also probably remember the day Dad brought us and our combined 100 silver dollars to the South Chicago Bank on Commercial so that we could have our own saving accounts, $50 each. You looked important and grown up at thirteen, so even though I hated turning over my silver stash, I figured it was a good thing because you proudly showed me your savings book after you had relinquished your collection."

"Yeah, on more than a couple of occasions, I wondered if Ida knew about Howard's modern move that erased her hard won gifts. We traded love for interest."

"I think my collecting silver all those years ago had something to do with what we lost. Ida, Mom. Those days, when we put our dimes toward trees for Israel, and every time we bought one, we could name a person to honor. Each time we brought in a dime, we put a little green stamp of a leaf on a picture of a tree, and then when all the branches on the tree had leaves on them, we'd get a card with the person's name we'd honored on it. I'm not naïve, Bicie. I know we can't go back, and now I wish I knew how to go forward."

(Element)

Science lesson on a cloudy afternoon. Words pouring down, soaking them all.

Umbrellas broken and spent, red and blue.

It's the dead I remember, in summer somewhere.

The dead to come, and the dead already there.

How did you get so brown, hill? How did you get the sun to settle down?

Against the odds, they swigged the blue and tumbled into a seaside haven.

The comic's ploy and plunder.

At last, and long, they remembered.

Strangely, in Paradise.

DREAM

Sometimes the unexpected happens. Not the slow even crawl of historical precedent, but a star slicing the night, making it look like morning has come. Earlier than expected. Brighter than expected. Healthier than expected. More beautiful than any one of us could have ever expected. Putting odds makers in their place, on the ground, with the rest of us, in awe. Then, this one star gathers others, and they file in, dropping off supplies, books, repairs, renovations. Parts of our brain we had not used before open up. The impossible appears probable.

Who would have guessed? From out of nowhere came peace. You could look down from small hills and high mountains at the scattered dwellings below—tents, skyscrapers, farmhouses, apartments—all over the planet, and see into them, as if one side had been removed, sectioned, for better viewing. Bright fires burning, in each one of them, but not out of control. They light up the ground below like the stars have managed above.

Seeing that light, my sister, Leah Liv Rubenstein Miller, decided to stay.

CODA

If I am not for myself, then who will be for me?
If I am only for myself, what am I?
And if not now, when?
—Rabbi Hillel

In the golden years, with all four of us together—Howard, Rosie, Leah, and me—lots of people thought Israel constituted a good back up plan, giving us a place to run, the next time Jew hatred whirled tornado-like over peaceful homes. Now Jew hatred whips at windows, but this time with a bitter, bitter twist. The land that would save us has become the beast that bites us. And now fully bereft, Leah and I still dream our parents' bodies back through the front door, the back door, *any* door. Our hearts, open and broken, catch at the sight of them, the thought of them. The golden age in our little family, past. The dream that Israel would shore up Jewish culture for Jews everywhere, stumbling.

Paradise is not the ancient land, which only I have visited and my sister still dreams of as a saving place. Instead, it's the constant knowing that no place can promise complete safety and you must move out into the scary blue anyway. It's the will to give up possession and the unholy fear that breeds it. It is that opening in the brain which only babies remember as they claw their way into forgetting, entering our world in sorrow for what they have lost.

I would like to say that I have finally become a lover of Israel or that Leah's attempt at understanding my terror of a Jewish homeland did not almost destroy her. I'd like to say I saved her, but she had already decided to live, the old Leah, the one who argues with me, the one who refuses "to believe in this fairy story of one land, many peoples," even if in a moment of inspired grace she conjured a memorable rendition of that tale. Since none of that has come to pass, I promise to look at love and terror and hold them both in my arms. I will hold all of it in my arms, if you, my beloveds, the living ones and the dead ones, will hold me in yours.

And, so, of course, they do. The living ones, at least. My old spirits have come to say good-bye, for good. They'd started weaning me a while ago, leaving me mostly ready for their departure.

So this is it, Danny?

Mija, *you forget, where I fly there is no "it," only infinite.*

So, my dear, as you can see, your friend the comic has now become the cleric.

Then even Emma waters up. Danny smiles. Edward, whom Danny coaxed along for the visit, leaves a few books in the room. Professor Said[*] has a lot to say, as people like to say. In the end, a lot about how the longing for a place could live folded inside a piece of music, and how that music could lift us all. If not here, then where? If not us, then how?

---

[*] Go look him up if you don't know.

Acknowledgments

Many thanks to those writers who encouraged me by example through their own work and in friendship with support for mine: Max Elbaum, Alma Luz Villanueva, Liz Zelvin, Louise Nayer, Abby Bogomolny, Avotcja, Jack Hirschman, Lisa Gale Garrigues, Daphne Muse, Moazzem Sheikh, Ernie Brill, David Spero, Diana Scott, Joel Schechter, and Aurora Levins Morales.

To my first reader, and daughter, Caya Schaan and second readers, and friends, Lauri Fried-Lee and Noemi Sohn, goes much gratitude for your patience and loving attention.

To Frances Goldin who believed in *The Divine Comic* early on and knew there was "a woman editor who would see its value," I will always be grateful. So thank you, Aurelia Lavalee for being that editor, and to t thilleman at Spuyten Duyvil for being willing to take a risk with this story.

To my teachers Louise Stanek, Beth Schultz, Barbara Christian, and Sue Schweick, who taught me how to read in ways I never could have imagined when I picked up my first book.

To colleagues and friends Ann Wettrich, Lauren Muller, Abdul Jabbar, Lijia Lumsden, Ruth Mahaney, Tina Martin, Anita Martinez, Jennifer Biehn, and Vivian Calderon who practice teaching and listening so well. To my students who teach me more than they will ever know.

To writer and filmmaker Allie Light whose heart and home are always open to artists and writers, I am honored to call you friend and to have counted among my friends and mentors your dear partner in love and art Irving Saraf. Thanks also to Irving's family in Israel.

To artists Yolanda Lopez, Miranda Bergman, Susan Greene, Juana Alicia, Judith Shaw, Billie Quijano, Tron Bykle, Winona Kirk, Wei Lin, and Beverly Toyu whose bravery propels me.

To Leanna Noble and Jean Ishibashi (Ish) who put up with what few others would call "my charm." To Hollis Stewart and Beto Saldamando, in solidarity. To the originals–Anna Williams Hayden, Kathy Sikora, Nancy Reder, Teddy Bofman, Peggy Kharroz, Aisha Kassahoun. To Wendy Lloyd, Rae Schiff, Phyl Soonachan, Herb Felsenfeld, and Gail Newman who get Passover. To Cecilia and Lalo Valdez for all those other meals. To my beloveds on the other side, Ellen Cohn (always, El), Notre Robinson Chatman, Rosemarie Hill, Agathe Bennich, Linda Rosa Corazon, Kathy Barisione, Tede Matthews, Marie Peckinpah, Dan Kirk, Lori Wong.

To Hilton Obenzinger, Lincoln Bergman, Gayle Markow, and others at the Jewish Alliance against Zionism (JAAZ) who allowed me to join forces with them to see another way.

To my guides at the Middle East Children's Alliance, Penny Rosenwasser and Mitchell Plitnick. To the Palestinian Writers Union and the Palestinian Center for the Study of Non-Violence. Your commitment to peace and justice continues to inspire me.

Thank you Tikva Parnas, Roni Ben-Efrat, Stephen Langfur, Maya Rosenfeld, and Carleen Gerber for sharing your experiences and expertise.

To our Seder regulars, brother Marc and sister-in-law Mary, their children, and grandchildren.

To daughter Caya, our healer; and son Sage, yes, our rock; their partners Natan and Blossom and the new generation they have blessed us with—Josiah Rowan, Cheveyo Eugene, Mateo Paz.

To Donny, for all the years and much more. This book would be nowhere without you.

LESLIE SIMON is the author of *Jazz/ is for white girls, too* (Poetry for the People), *i rise/ you riz/ we born* (Artaud's Elbow), *High Desire* (Wingbow Press), and *Collisions and Transformations* (Coffee House Press). She co-authored (with Jan Johnson Drantell) *A Music I No Longer Heard: The Early Death of a Parent* (Simon and Schuster). She has published essays on film, literature, and politics and teaches at City College of San Francisco.

CPSIA information can be obtained
at www.ICGtesting.com
Printed in the USA
FSHW012131040122
87407FS